Underground Chronicles: The Payment

David Baldwin

Jahphut
Washington, D.C.

Published 2005
Published by Jahphut, P.O. Box 2540, Washington DC
20013, USA

thepayment@jahphut.com

This book is a work of fiction. Names, Characters, places
and incidents either are products of the Authors imagination
or are used fictitiously. Any resemblance to actual events or
locales or persons, living or dead is entirely coincidental.

ISBN 0-9770630-2-X

Printed in the United States of America

I thank The Almighty and his Hosts. I also would like to thank the English staff at Ballou Senior High School for reiterating that my gift was real. And special thanks to Cathy Simon for taking a pile of papers with no punctuations and turning it into a pool of red ink. It was those red marks that showed me how to express myself, so you could understand. I would also like to thank my families from Washington, DC, Pennsylvania, Virginia, Maryland, North Carolina and Ohio. It's too many of you to name. Love you continuously!

For My Mother,
Patricia Louise

Chapter

1

A Thought
to Remember

Compare my neighborhood to the Wild West, where the pursuit of freedom and gold had many deadly consequences. In my hood, as it was at the great frontier, cowboys, gangsters and soldiers ruled. In both places, good persistence was confused with bad intentions and bad intentions confused with good persistence. Whichever side, good or bad, war was the means by which the victor's will was imposed.

The gun was the balancing act. In the West and in my hood it tipped the scales, as it transformed cowards into brave men and brave men into dead ones. War was its grand stage.

The fighting introduced itself as an ambush, sometimes planned as a drive-by or a kidnapping, complete with duct tape.

I don't compare it to the great battles fought by the Screaming Eagles at Bastogne or the Zulu fighters against the Red Coats at Isandlwana or even at Kambula. And I don't liken it to the Civil War and those legendary sacrifices.

No, this war was an all-out assault for one city block. On

the same block where my boys and I played marbles and
pitched pennies, we grew up to wreak havoc on the
community and on our world.

Like the bandit holding the saloon captive, these were
the times when "law and order" were dreamed about and
justice cried for. Those days have revisited us here in the
winding hills and dirt paths of Southeast Washington, D.C.,
where our fathers have disappeared without a trace and our
mothers cry out for justice.

My mind drifted when I heard the news that day, as I
headed to class. I was told that Melvin Bell was killed after a
basketball game the day before. I began to see images of him
skating at the rink like an old time derby skater, doing back
jumps and three sixties, all while shaking his hands,
gesturing in the way of a gambler. I saw him doing the
Happy Feet, the Freak, break dancing and having a good
old-fashioned time at the weekend ranking party.

An amateur reporter uncovered that bets were set on a
game and Melvin came off with the wages.

Melvin was a gambling fanatic. As a matter of fact, the
last time I saw him, we were in the lavatory betting my last
two dollars.

I lowered my head and shook it in remembrance of his
life. I wondered about the scene and the seconds before he
died. Did he get a chance to say, no? Did he ask for a chance
to see another day or to smell the air from the face of the
waters?

I took to the halls looking for my man Ant to tell him
about Melvin. Ant was probably ducking me since I crushed
him in Playstation's John Madden last night. I flowed
through the halls with my hat tilted and my scarf wrapped
around my neck, looking like an airplane pilot out of the

"Happy Days" era. I cased the school like I owned it. This was my eleventh grade year at Ballou Senior High. As I strolled down the hall, I ran into Principal Hawkins and he told me to take my hat off and to get to class — and to class I went.

In my favorite class, my history teacher, Mr. Binshem, was preparing to play the role of Peter, one of Benjamin Franklin's black male servants. Mr. B often portrayed people like Martin Luther King, Jr., Abraham Lincoln and he even did an African King named Ndombe. According to him, they were people who had giant impacts on our history and he portrayed them to give us a better perspective of the past.

"I've been catapulted here to the twentieth century to experience the great vindication and transformation, and to give you some sense," Peter said. "Fortunately," he continued, "I am happy to see you wipe-out xenophobia from the ignorant-pure with the hand of patience and truth."

Mr. Binshem had black curly hair. He looked like Richard Gere in the movie *King David*. Mr. B. played the part of Peter very well even down to his tattered pants and patchy shirt. At times, it looked like he was clowning people, but the truth of it was, he just could not act.

"Take out your assignment. I have a question," Peter started. "The carriages that go about the streets, how is that without horses?"

"What carriages?" my classmate and buddy, Ronald asked.

"The cars," I whispered.

The assignment he asked us to take out was a take-home quiz about Benjamin Franklin and electricity.

"While I check the quiz, I want you to write a correspondence to Queen Elizabeth and tell her about your life and don't forget to ask her for something. She is the queen, you know, the great mother."

I wrote:

"Great Mother, Queen Elizabeth: My friend got killed last night. Well, he's not really my best friend. He is a good friend. He got shot in the head. We have some bloody sidewalks; a lot of people get killed around here. I see you on horses sometimes when I watch the news. I think you the Queen of America. We just your nephews and nieces of them brothers and sisters who broke away. My little sister gets on my nerve. See ya."

"Next assignment," he said, as he began to write on the blackboard, "is to find out how a motor operates and the importance of electricity to it."

"He goin' to slave us to death!" Ronald said.

"I am no slave. I am a black male servant," Peter said, looking agitated.

"Ok, tell us. What are you, Peter?" I asked.

"Humble yourselves! You must understand that a student learns and works from lessons given by the teacher. I, being your teacher at that moment, became your master," he said, "and these things students are based on order and respect. Now, let's go to lessons. We dealt with my master becoming a master printer last week."

"Not again! Do we have to talk about Benjamin Franklin again?" Ronald asked indignantly.

"But such is history, the mother of this rewarding existence," he said, as forceful as a preacher at the lectern.

"*His* story maybe," someone uttered.

"Benjamin Franklin," he said excitedly. "Ok, you like money; he's the one with his face on the hundred dollar bill. Yeah, it was he who experimented with electricity and almost died from such experiments. He did the research on units he called the electrical-battery more than two hundred and fifty years ago. And guess what? The carriages of today have an electrical battery."

"He has told me many things and has allowed me to read

books and to travel when many of my race," his voice cracked as he continued, "was forbidden to do such things." He closed his eyes and stood there still and silent.

I thought Benjamin Franklin was one of the greatest humans God had ever produced and it wasn't because he created bifocal glasses or because he suggested John Carroll to Papal Nuncio for the organization of the Roman Catholic Church in America. It wasn't even because he created the University of Pennsylvania or the fact that he freed Peter in the 1760s. My thought was if it wasn't for him, I wouldn't have been playing PlayStation, and that was something I couldn't imagine.

Ronald slipped me a note, asking did I hear about Melvin. I gestured, yes. We looked at each other and just shook our heads. There we were, two teenagers totally confused.

Yet, at that fruitful age the value of human life was a thought less considered.

I asked him had he seen Ant that morning.

He said, "No."

Chapter 2

Craps

On the home set my sister was yapping her chops on the phone, sitting on the La-Z-Boy and watching the Flintstones. The phone had to be an extension of her arm. Every time I saw her, the phone wasn't far away. What do her and her friends talk about all day long? I thought they talked about Christmas-land and the Circus community.

It was like that movie *The Nightmare before Christmas*, only there was no nightmare. Every time the phone touched her ear, she got very euphoric. She told me granddad called and wanted me to go to the corner store.

I called my man Ant and told him to be outside in twenty minutes. I went downstairs where granddad lived, which was very convenient for him, especially when he needed someone to go to the store. Most people called him "Captain Buck."

He was also known as "The Old Man." I called him "Buck" or "Granddad

"What you need?" I asked.

"A drink!" he said chuckling. "You know you're in Federal City now, boy. That's right. They're about to take this city." This was the year Marion Barry bowed out, the year Pope John Paul II visited Cuba and the year Peyton Manning was the NFL's number-one draft pick.

"Who 'bout to take the city?" I asked.

"The Control Board," he said, looking at the baseball section in the Washington Post. "They're trying to take the city."

"I can't help wit' that, but I could get ya somethin' from the store."

"Marion Barry will be back," he said, "just like baseball and a... did you finish that book yet?"

"Uh uh," I answered. He was talking about the book by Robert B. Edgerton *Like Lions They Fought*.

"What's taking you so long. You need to read and pay attention in about five year's time Southeast wont look the same?"

"I've been kind of busy," I said.

Buck gave me twenty dollars for every book I read. The only catch was it had to be a book he picked out.

The first book outside of fairytale land, that had more than twenty pages was Gordon Parks' *Voices in the Mirror*.

Gordon Parks, a great man by the highest standards, dealt with racism in his life and in his community that I didn't experience in my hood. In my hood, we ruled; and all our leaders were black, save one — and he was the President. President Clinton had big love in our hood. If it wasn't for my grandfather, I would have never heard of the great Gordon Parks.

"Get me a glass out the cabinet and hand me that there bottle... You need to finish them books. I got more."

I handed him the bottle of Seagram's Gin that was sitting on the end table. He got ice out the fridge.

"Now, that there's a man's drink, boy!" he said confidently. "You need something from the store?"

"Why you young people so rushy, rushy? I mean, just

can't wait a minute. That there is y'all problem, you know. If you just sit back and enjoy time and life, you might just learn something. Naw, you just too strong for ya own good, just jumping, just jumping. That's right, y'all just...."

"Excuse me, Granddad!" I interrupted.

"See," he continued, as he took another drink. "See, just jumping, rushy, rushy. Where ya have to go?"

"Pooh said you wanted somethin' from the store," I answered.

"Take a seat," he said. "What you into boy? You need to be in those books I gave you," he said, chewing his gum. "I know you into something. The Orioles might do something this year... You into them girls, boy?"

"They all right," I answered, rubbing my head, grinning. He started laughing again.

"I saw a little belle today, boy. Yeah, she looked so sweet, like we could play checkers or something too."

"Yeah?" I asked.

He nodded his head, grinning. "I think she likes me."

"Oh yeah?"

"L," a voice shouted. "Larnell!"

It was my man Ant. As I headed for the door, I shook my head thinking, *I can't believe Buck is still looking at women.*

My grandmother passed five years ago and it was the worst time of my life. It was the first time someone close had died. I remember I couldn't get myself together. I thought God took the sun away and turned all flowers to ashes. All my beautiful thoughts about life turned to thoughts of death. Her death shook my whole soul for what felt like eternity. And when it stopped, I had one thought— "I will never fall in love with this life."

She was the love and support that held the family together. Everything reminded me of her lifeless body. Our coffee table was her coffin and every song that came on the radio was the wrong song.

I hated each and every tune without even considering the lyrics. Songs like Elvis Presley's *"In The Ghetto,"* a beautiful song by all accounts, but I hated it.

"What up?" I asked Ant.

"They said niggas on the hill killed Melvin," Ant said.

"I wonder why though?" I asked.

"He probably broke their ass. You know them jealous niggas."

"Over nickels and dimes?"

"Yeah, over dimes, son," Ant said.

"Crazy!" I said, trying to make sense out of it.

"I am broke as a bastard right now," Ant said.

"Shouldn't have spent all your money up in G-town."

"Ask your peeps to hook us up," Ant said.

He was talking about my cousin Julius givin' us some work.

"Hook us up with what?" I asked.

"Look, your folks run this joint. I'm tired of being broke. I'm tryin' to put some Jacksons in my pockets, know what I mean? Benjamins an' shit," Ant said, low in spirit.

"I don't see it. I don't see him giving us nothing but a couple of coins."

"How you know if you haven't talked to him?"

"Man talkin' bout Benjamins, you talkin' Playstation. You ever think bout that?"

"What... Who?"

"That's Mr. Electricity, the reason why churches and houses don't burn down from lighting anymore."

"What?!" Ant said, frustrated. "That's dreamland shit."

"The man created..."

"Naw," Ant interrupted, "you just scared. What Benjamin Franklin got to do with talkin' to your peeps?"

"Ok, I got to repeat myself. HE-IS-NOT-GOING-TO-GIVE-US- ANYTHING," I said, moving my hands as I enunciated each word because his ears didn't understand it coming out of my mouth, and I knew that.

"You scared of your mother?"

"If you didn't spend all your money up Georgetown, you might have money in your pocket," I said.

"Yeah, yeah, you right. But right now, I'm broke and we got to find another way. I am tired of stealing Jimmy Dean sausages for Ms. Parker."

"She owe us twenty for the last drop." I said.

"Man, that's still not enough. I mean look at these guys like Arthur, Randle and Larry. They got our issue… Man, that's your cuz."

"They don't have our issue. They gettin' money like we got to get," I said.

"That's why you got to talk to your folks. But right now I need a sucker who is willing to bet some coins."

"I got the dice right here," I said. I proceeded to shake those joints to a dancer's rhythm and the rhyme went click-click, thumb to the index finger.

We dropped off my grandpa's milk and bread and went to the circle. If you wanted action, the circle is where you wanted to be. Twenty-four six-story buildings surrounded the yard.

The Mayor, Steve, was there.

We called him the Mayor because he knew everybody in the hood. He always smelled like he needed a little water on his body. He didn't change his clothes much. Rock was there also, looking idle as a docked boat. I asked him had he seen Julius or Larry and he said no. Julius was my first cousin. His father, Uncle Charles, was my mother's oldest brother.

Uncle Charles was serving a twenty-year sentence for racketeering and murder.

Nine times out of ten you would see Rock in the circle. We couldn't get him to bet. He maintained himself outside of the clusters but was always around.

We stayed there for a while looking for bettors. Ant was

calling the bettors out as I thumbed the dice in my hand.

In the moon's presence, three guys gently slipped between the buildings toward us.

It was like a covert sting in a best-selling spy thriller. I didn't recognize their walks or their aggressive and penetrating silhouettes.

"Y'all know them?" Rock asked, as he moved counter to their advance.

"Naw!" Ant responded.

"What's up fellas?" Steve said.

"Me looking for Julius?" one guy said with an accent I couldn't discern.

"Not here," Rock responded. "What you need?"

"Julius!" the foreigner repeated.

"I'm looking for him, too," I said.

"You tell him me Mag."

"Right, right, but not here. Can I help you with something?" Steve asked.

"Me Mag and you?" he asked Steve.

"Oh! Y'all need to go. He ain't here." Rock said, annoyingly.

"Tell him me Mag, and I'd like to see him".

"Right, right. He likes his name," Steve said.

"What about it?" Rock asked.

"Julius and me have business," the Mag said.

"Where you from man?" Ant asked, with noticeable irritation.

"Around, up the block," he said.

"Not here!" Rock yelled. "You need to be gone." He continued with his hands moving frantically about as he moved back and forth like a caged lion. The emotions in the atmosphere rose. One guy with Mag put his hands in his pullover sweatshirt. It was too dark to tell whether or not he was gripping the steel equalizer.

"Yeah, be gone!" Ant said, also vexed with the answer

offered, began to take on an offensive mood as well.

"No hostility," Mag said, "Julius is our business."

"Well, he ain't here," Rock said.

"No hostility. Me come back."

"Your best bet!" Rock said.

Mag, seemingly understanding the situation in which he had put himself, left with tensions piercing the roof.

"Did somebody say bet? I think I heard somebody say bet. Did somebody say bet?" I asked, trying to crack the thick smoke in Ant's and my favor. I saw that the block had filled up with a few low-wage bettors. It was all about economics when we entered the circle. Two heads jumped at the chance to get at our coins. I shook the dice to a bet of five dollars. With a twist, I rolled the dice onto the stones passing and hit numbers.

Those bones felt like an appendage. It was me against the stones as I drifted in the gambler's zone.

The stones gave numbers, as I bounced the twins across them, looking to hit, feeling a hit. I was in the zone; even Las Vegas couldn't indulge this thirst. As the betting increased to fifteen dollars, Ant placed side bets of twenty and jointly we won a hundred and sixty-five dollars.

In one of the poorest neighborhoods in America, we shuffled monies back and forth.

It was like the carpeted craps tables in Atlantic City. The bets got bigger with players laying down fifties and hundreds. Players shaking and rolling the twin bones on the stones. Players with two hundred-dollar leather jackets and eighty-dollar tennis shoes took this game for life and death.

I began to think about Melvin's death, thinking that by these means he lost his life. I wondered about the actual numbers and the purse.

This heart-pumping, anxiety-filled sport can take it all away, like it took Melvin's life. Craps is one of the ways we make our ends and exchange currency. "Time to blow this joint," I said, as our game was up in their pockets.

The midnight scales measured gracefully for Ant and me. Earnings from this kind of activity paid for our self-esteem. We were still looking for it subconsciously in our everyday lives.

"Value is added at half a penny," Captain Buck would say.

Julius finally pulled up in his Fleetwood. His world seemed to move slower than the rest of ours. Violent summer storms didn't cover the sun's rays on him. His actions played on movie scenes. As he got out his car, the world slowed and paid attention. The gold on his neck and about his fingers was in accord with the living elements. With Wembo, his main man Larry, and Don Don at his side, he approached the circle.

"Yo Ant, check him out," I said, referring to Larry. "See if he got some coins to lose."

"Numbers baby, numbers. Come on five. Come on!" I summoned the dice.

"Eh, Don Don, Larry, bet them ends?" Ant asked.

"What you bettin'?" Larry asked.

"Point is five man. What you got?"

"Ain't no good. He on next one. Gimme that!" I said, as I hit the point.

"Three hundred on the point," I said, as I looked up at my cousin Julius and gave him a head nod.

Don Don jumped out there and dropped fifteen twenties. He was one of Julius's friends who had business up the block.

"Bet," he said.

"I'll side that for two," Larry said.

"Bet," Ant said.

I've never been that hot on the twins. This was the first time I was up more than a hundred sixty dollars. Gambling for quarters and dimes had progressed to that level. Ant and

I would have bet it all for the big pay out. The dice came out and settled on nine.

"Nina," I said, as I gave the patent twist.

Ant in the background said, "Do your thing, dog."

"Nina."

"Do your thing, dog."

"Come on Nina. He don't want it," I said. "Nina!"

"What's up with them, jumping out there like that?" Larry asked Julius.

"Show him, L," Ant uttered.

"Nina, come to Daddy," I said, as I brought the shake up high about the ears. "I hear ya. I love ya. Come on Nina, come on. Yes! It came sweet. Nina, it came sweet. I love you, sweetie."

The next day, I could not wait until school was over. After second period I had reconditioned myself to the nothingness and prepared myself for the day's exit. Then the real learning began.

"What's up, Ant?"

"I am fucked up about Melvin," Ant said, as we proceeded toward our lockers.

"Yo, I heard they took his Tag-Heuer watch and then hit him with two to the head. The more I hear about it, the madder I get," I said.

"Petty busters gonna get theirs," Ant said.

"Yeah, I know. Let's go up to Georgetown?" I said.

"Yeah," Ant said. You talk about me and spending."

My eyes quickly focused on the beauty walking down the hall… my beauty. Her name was Robin.

"Hey! What's up, girl?"

"You know my name," she replied swiftly.

"Why the hostility?" I asked.

"You didn't call last night."

"It got too late."

"I don't want to hear that."

"I missed something. When y'all get married?" Ant asked.

"Forget you, Ant."

"It's like that because I didn't call you last night."

"Let's roll, Larnell," Ant said.

"All right, man. look, I'll call you later," I said. She looked up and rolled her eyes. "I'll call you later," I repeated as I turned to walk away.

I didn't understand the importance of school and I was still learning how to deal with the opposite sex.

I was told school was for training and the place where you acquired understanding. Well, my school was far from that for me.

The only thing enlightening about it was the young ladies and history. And that's where I directed my focus— to study and love, respectively. My granddaddy told me that women were the most sacred creators under the heavens. I wasn't sure about that though. Some of the things Robin got mad about didn't even make sense. So, how can someone who doesn't make sense be sacred?

We jumped on the 32 Friendship Heights bus to the heart of Georgetown.

Georgetown was of a different culture. It was a place where men of persuasion made deals for good fashion and precious metals.

It was the fashion market, the upper crust market, the historical market and the educational market all rolled into one. The consistency of its architecture shouted of integrity.

"My family is from Georgetown," I said to Ant.

"After the Civil War my great grandparents migrated to Georgetown in the Foggy Bottom area."

"Oh, yeah?"

"Yeah, they sold the property for big bucks."

"Right. So they could move to Southeast?"

"I guess."

"My folks are from Philly."

"My grandfather came down from Philly when he was young. Benjamin Franklin came from there too," I said.

"Who cares?" Ant said, shrugging his shoulders.

The buildings in the hood were uninspiring, red square monsters. But it didn't make a difference. We didn't know architecture or the story behind the stones.

Georgetown's story is very rich. It has America's oldest Catholic University. Georgetown was named in honor of King George II. I was drawn to it when the Georgetown Hoyas won the Final Four. I was young then, but I remember the excitement. John Thompson and the Hoyas had the basketball world buzzing and inner city D.C. loved it.

With Ant, I went there to spend money. We frequented the old ground for a little trade. Our favorite store by far was Prince and Princess. It had the nice boots, leathers, tennis shoes and all the top favored garments around. And we knew the owner, Faprilo, very well. Every time we broke a crap game we were up Georgetown and in his store.

"How much for two pair?" Ant asked.

"One seventy," answered Faprilo.

"There you go. Why you treatin' me like that? I come in here and spend money," Ant said.

"Anywhere else you get for ninety; eighty-five is me price," Faprilo said.

Ant was clearly disappointed. While he looked at Faprilo, his lips and nose took on an aggressive posture. Yet, he knew Faprilo was going to stick to his price

Faprilo was hard on the one-item shoppers. He maintained that their prices were already discounted. But, as always we came to spend. The more we spent, the more we saved. That's the old-fashioned way of purchasing. Bringing the ethics of the wholesale market down to the retail market was a sweet blessing.

We didn't have to pay top dollar, but we sure did look like we did. During those times, it was our clothes that provided onlookers with a message that we deserved honor and respect.

Our clothes were fresh and the respect and admiration we received from our peers compensated for the abnegate feelings predominate in the hood.

"I need a pair of New Balance and an outfit. Do somethin' for me," Ant said to Faprilo.

"Pick an outfit and we'll see," Faprilo responded.

Moments later a young lady entered the store and gracefully walked past me. You couldn't tell me I didn't see air and smell glass. That's right; I said *"glass."* Everything was understood. *It must be a crime for someone to be so fine,* I thought.

She walked meticulously across my scope and asked Faprilo about tennis skirts. She was nice and fly. I mean seriously, she was like sweet honey at the good harvest celebration. Her hair was in African twists and her blue jeans were fitted rank and file. Faprilo told her, they didn't have anymore tennis skirts. I had to say something. It was like a voice being audible for the ear; she was there for a reason.

"Do I know you?" I quickly blurted.

"I don't think so," she answered.

"How about we change all that," I said.

"No, I have a boyfriend."

"Even better. What's your name anyway?"

"Kim."

"Kim?" Ant said, looking befuddled. "I think I know you from somewhere."

"Where Ant?" I asked.

"Yeah, where you know me from?" she inquired.

It was unclear to Ant where he had known her from. He probably didn't know her at all.

"I got enough male friends," she said.

"One more won't hurt the situation," I said. I managed to give her my number before we navigated to the exit. Ant got his shoes, two outfits and on top of that, he paid seventy dollars instead of eighty-five for the pair of tennis shoes.

"She was tight for real," I said.

"I know her from somewhere, man. I'm tellin' you."

"I would love to sit on her couch and get to know her. I think I'm in love again."

"You always say that."

"Yeah, and I always crush you in PlayStation and what! Just for that, next time you pick those sorry Cowboys, we bettin' a hundred and fifty push-ups."

"In your dreams."

Chapter
3

The
Interrogation

Walking to school, I felt winter's solstice fade as the warmth of spring's beauty began to shine through. Things change when the rays of Sir Radiant start to pound. Buds of all sorts come forth to enjoy the light and energy. Colors from Salvia, Marigolds and Amaranths dominate the landscapes as greens maintain the parkways.

I felt like a young Tutankhamen as I entered my English class, gold about my neck and the red-striped Adidas' Top Tens protecting my soles. Chicks were cutting their eyes and guys acknowledging with a nod of their domes. *Yeah*! I thought.

The class was asked to pull out Emily Bronte's *Wuthering Heights*. Ronald was picked to read paragraph two of chapter three.

He began to read and his breath pattern began to crack. He was hyperventilating like a broken soldier in the heat of battle.

The words coming from his mouth were choking him. Beads of sweat took residence on his forehead. Anguish had over taken him.

"Slow down," the teacher said. The objective penned on the board read, "Learning how to get to a paragraph from a sentence."

Ronald stopped reading. The chuckles from the class helped shame take its hold.

"Continue reading," the teacher said. The only sound from Ronald was his breathing. I only hope she didn't call my name. I didn't want to battle with the stone and case iron desk. The learning board highlighted words that aimed to give me a headache.

It seemed like the radiator was throwing microwave fists. Certainly, this was the reason Ronald was sweating. His own voice turned against him, cracking and stumbling on every word. "Who needs such pain and humiliation?" I thought.

"Please excuse this interruption," the school's loud intercom ejected. "Larnell Kenneth, please report to the main office. Larnell Kenneth to the main office!"

I closed my eyes and shook my head. My fellow students looked at me like a tasty piece of the Colonel's best. Oddly enough this seemed to add to my self-esteem.

My name called over the loud speaker was equal to me being a star of a movie.

My mind began to race back over the morning. "What I do now?" I grunted.

The open doors in the learning areas helped with the illusion of worth. As I walked to the office, students and teachers alike were acknowledging that my presence made a difference. I was directed to Mr. Hawkins' office.

"Have a seat, Larnell!" Mr. Hawkins demanded, standing to the left of his desk near the back window. Sitting on the right corner was a police officer.

"How are you, Mr. Kenneth?" the officer asked.

"Cool", I answered.

"Larnell, the officer is here to ask you a few questions."

"Oh, yeah?"

"Yeah", the officer interrupted. "I am here investigating a murder, the murder of a Mr. Melvin Bell," he said, pulling out his notepad.

"I don't know nothin'," I said.

"I didn't ask what you knew," he said, in his official police voice.

"Mel was cool with me is all I'm sayin'."

"Look, I ask the questions, you answer the questions," the cop said. "Now, where were you Wednesday around ten o'clock?"

"At home," I answered.

"Do you have any idea why someone would kill Melvin?"

"No."

"Do you recall threatening him the day you both were suspended?"

The cop was trying to stunt me with that question. Melvin was my boy; I wouldn't intimidate Melvin in any way. I couldn't remember in detail what happened a week prior and the cop kept asking, "Do you remember? Do you remember?"

"Oh, you remember!" Mr. Hawkins said.

"I don't know nothing!" I shouted.

The cop started an inquiry on my personal life. He asked for my address, parents' names and names of my closest friends.

"I don't know nothing, didn't know about it until yesterday."

"You play dice, son?"

Do I play dice, I thought. Mr. Hawkins knew I shot dice, so I knew the officer was aware of it. A few weeks ago Melvin and I were caught in the boys' bathroom shooting dice for two dollars, but I didn't kill him.

"I be around it, trying to get a little issue," I said.

"Did you owe Melvin some money?"

"No."

"Did Melvin owe you some money?"

"No, I'm kind of pissed off about it myself." I said.

"I didn't ask you what you were pissed about. I am here on official police business. Answer the question that's asked."

"You got the wrong guy. Can I go back to class!"

"We'll tell you when to go to class," Mr. Hawkins said, sternly.

"Son, whatever you're hiding will come to light," the officer said, in a composed kind of way.

"Larnell, you have demonstrated no concept of right and wrong. You think this world is made for you and by you. Every day you and your crew have problems with the rules of this place. You are headed toward jail or death, if you don't get yourself together. Now, tell this officer the truth. Stop lying, son."

What truth! He really believes I killed Melvin. How does wearing my hats inside the school and walking to the left instead of the right make me a murderer?

"You going to tell us something!" the officer said.

"Look, I don't know nothin'. Can I go to class?" I asked, as I stood up.

"Sit back down boy!" the officer said, walking toward me.

If he didn't see the fire in my eyes, I sure felt it in my heart. I thought, as soon as he lifts his hands to touch me, I am going to grab the wooden chair and break it over his head.

But like a cheetah, his hands thrust toward my neck, subduing me in the seat. His left hand was about my neck as his right hand was slamming handcuffs on the chair and me.

"I'll break your neck, you little punk!" he said. "Now, I am here to find out who the fuck killed Melvin. And I will find out who did it, got damn it. Do you understand that, boy?"

"Larnell, I heard you threaten that young man," Mr.

Hawkins asserted. "I was right there. Let's say you remember, it doesn't mean you killed him. But you did say it, didn't you? Didn't you?" Mr. Hawkins asked, looking at me with his patent leather roach killers and a tie knotted so big it looked liked a clip-on.

"I don't know what you're talkin' about." I said.

"You fuckin' punk. If I find out you had anything to do with this killing, you will wish for death," the officer said.

Deep down in the ghetto townships of Washington D.C., where the descendants of an unlearned people live, ignorance is the first of many deadly obstacles. This is the town where there were more than 4,000 unsolved murders and the owner of the professional basketball team changed the name from the Washington Bullets to the Washington Wizards because of his love for the citizens in the city.

Choking me and handcuffing me was the style of interrogation, but was it against the law?

This was the time I wished for my missing father. However, in a community where law wasn't acknowledged on either flank, chaos ran its course unabated.

"He was cool with me," I said, with a tear rolling over the lower eyelid.

"Cry, you fake punk. Cry on and tell mommy," the officer said.

"I ain't crying."

"What do you know about it, son?" The officer continued, as if the story in my lips had changed course, when he saw the tear.

The words going through my mind were rumbling like thunder, but all I could say was, "May I go to class now?" as I pulled up on the chair and handcuffs.

"Look at him," Mr. Hawkins said. "I heard what he said, the little lying trouble maker."

"Ok, I'll be calling you again and if I as much as catch you spitting, I will throw you in jail," the officer said as he released me from the chair. As soon as I walked out of the office tears began to flow down like a giant crack at an old dam. I decided not to go back to class.

I slipped through the school's kitchen door, climbed the fence and broke out the gate for the neighborhood. I couldn't believe shooting dice for pennies and walking on the left side of the halls had equaled a murderous personality. I screamed, real loud, and started to run home.

I pulled and grabbed at my body to remove all thoughts of restraint. I ran and ran. I passed the older men loitering in front of the liquor stores. One of them could be my father. That's why cops could slam handcuffs on me and get away with it. That's why, because my father was drunk in front of the spirits store and begging for pennies.

"I hate you. I hate you!" I yelled.

I wasn't sure if I was talking to Officer Thunderbutt or the men aimlessly loitering for the sake of freedom. As my anger gave way to exhaustion, I noticed Julius gesturing me to him. He was posted on his car.

"What's wrong with you?" he asked.

I couldn't wait to tell him what had happened. After rattling off my story, he said, "Well, that kind of stuff happens around here kid. You were huffing and puffing like you had real drama or something."

"That was real, the officer putting his finger all in my face. He took the strap off his gun," I said, regaining my breath.

"So, did you do it?"

"No!"

"Why are you so excited?"

"Because it's all messed up. That nigga didn't have too…it's all messed up."

"What is?"

"They don't have a right…"

"Well," he interrupted, "the lines between right and

wrong are very thin around here, but I'll tell you what. I know just what you need."

"What's that?"

"You need an exotic woman friend about now. Have you ever had a good rub down?"

I said, "No."

"Let's ride, then." We wheeled onto Interstate 495.

"Those women do things to you that make you want to live forever. Know what I mean?" he said excitedly.

"Like what?" I couldn't imagine some of the stuff he said could or would ever happen to me. Some of it sounded like bacteria waiting to grow. We pulled up at White Flint Mall. He went to Marshall's and pulled out the biggest roll of currency I had ever seen in my life.

Twenties rolled off like a ton of grapefruits on a hill that peaks at ninety degrees. This was an impression unmatched. Learning how to make money like that was a goal worth seeking.

"Where is your man Ant?" he asked.

"School," I answered. "Eh Julius," I started to ask him to put Ant and me on the bankroll, but stopped short and switched gears to something a little more serious. "Did they tell you about that dude Mag?"

"Yeah, Rock told me about him and I still don't know who he was."

"He said something about business, but things almost got out of hand."

"That's easy."

"What?" I asked not fully understanding what he meant.

"You got to be cautious," he said. "Hey," he continued, seemingly evading the topic, "do you want something from here?"

"Yeah, you right," I said.

We were in the casual sport section at Hecht's department store.

Julius had on some gray alligator shoes and a pair of black slacks with a red shirt.

"Hey, we need some help here," he called, "I'd like to see my little cousin in some nice jeans, some dirty bucks, and good shirt. He had a rough day, you know what I mean," Julius said to the clerk.

I came out the store with two hundred dollars worth of clothes. He bought me some Bass shoes, a pair of Ralph Lauren jeans and a few shirts.

"You could wear jeans two or three days in a row, you feel me?" he asked.

"Not really," I answered. I wasn't into wearing the same clothes.

"Just think about it. Who cares? They're all blue. But they'll definitely notice shirts."

He could take this argument to someone else. I didn't plan on ever wearing the same jeans day after day. I had to be fresh at all costs.

"See, with me I don't wear tennis shoes. I move in shoes or boots. I don't play a lot of sports, so I have no need for them. I was born a Mack. I run my game as I please," Julius said, with conviction.

As we walked through the mall, I noticed stores that specialized in diamonds and gold, "homeland items," as Buck would say.

America's favorite boutiques and outlets with top fashion had signs that glittered like gold. Stores like Macy's and Nordstrom's running the land and the mall wanted merchandise. All this seemed so great and grand. But does it all equal out to a big game? People smiled in the corridors as the cash registers rang the bells of - freedom; so glorious and most precious.

Yet, earlier that day, I ran home in rage, removing the chains that held me to the wooden chair. I tried in vain, to remove the chains that held me down to the scraps of nourishment and knowledge. The recipe for destruction was sweet as grandma's Kool-Aid.

Blood stained the concrete where Melvin took his last breath and you wonder, did the world stop for a moment? The modern day bandits are known for killing and intimidation, and they use the same tools that bandits used in the frontier days. Lawlessness aided their cause. The mascot for the community was the pirate. It symbolized the standard.

What we wanted was the glitter and gold. This eased all distress, even if only for the moment. It was understood instinctively that tomorrow would be taken care of.

I know I didn't have any thought of the matters for the day ahead.

Money blinded me for the moment. I enjoyed trying on the new clothes, looking in the mirror and saying, "Like that!" Kings and queens didn't dress in rags. To look my best made me feel I was the best. What else could it be but the pursuit of money and happiness? Julius had demonstrated this. I mean, as we walked the mall, people knew him. Sporting a real face he said, "I am what I am."

I don't think he graduated from elementary school, let alone high school. His means to an end was him and his work. The ends he peeled from the bank roll he toted was like a great mountain. Many would desire to conquer but few will ever attain.

"You know what I mean?" Julius asked, as he pimp walked his way though the halls of the mall. "I am what I am and I don't play tennis."

"I don't play tennis either," I said. I didn't even know that tennis shoes were for tennis. My tennis shoes, were not for sports. My top ten Adidas were part of my uniform and a major part of my flavor, but on the box they came in, the label indicated they were for basketball.

It would take me two to three months to consider

playing basketball in them. By then, they would have a few scuff marks.

"I don't play sports in my new tennis," I said.

"That's why they are a waste," he replied.

"I don't agree," I said.

"You'll see what I mean," he said.

"Look, you have on those slippery joints. If something break out, I could run in my tennis and all you're goin' to do is slip and slide. I don't have time to slip and slide."

He got a little laugh off of that. "Look little cuz," he said, "if something breaks, I ain't doing no running. Ducking and dodging is one thing, but running is out."

"Sometimes you got to run," I said.

"Not me. Just to fight another day? I don't want to fight another day. Motherfuckers have no reason to even think they want to deal on those terms," he said earnestly.

We stopped at the Subway sandwich shop and got down on a couple of turkey and cheese sandwiches.

"War is out there and you're going to have to get ready." "War?" I asked, confused.

"Yeah, your man Melvin got killed because of the war."

He got up and with great force slapped the corner of a table where two white guys were sitting.

"What's up?" Julius asked.

"Hey guy," one guy returned. The guy who spoke had on a sports jacket and his hair looked like corn silk. He stood up and shooked Julius's hand.

Julius sat down and began to talk. The conversation tone went under the audible range.

What in the world does he have in common with these guys, I thought. Their facial expressions were serious, but not aggressive. Julius listened intently as he rubbed his goatee.

Chapter
4

The
Introduction

Julius turned on Interstate 495, the Capitol Beltway, the bounds of the Capitol City. We moved with the rhythm and precision of Northstar in his '98 Cadillac Brougham and the pavement was smooth. The road flowed past.

The sightseeing cruisers and visitors in the slow lanes, we flowed past. Exit signs to upscale communities and hotels, we flowed past. The Temptations' voices and music played on our pulses. The song *"Ball of Confusion"* went through Julius' head. He rocked back and forth as the sun's glory was beaming; the road moving as the car bounced; the red glow glared off the window.

The Temptations had the stage, with voices going high low and everywhere. We just rode. The road and the car were one.

"..and the band played on…" Julius sung, as he rocked to the beat.

"Do you have a girlfriend?" Julius asked.

"Nope," I answered.

"Well, that's not too bad. You'll have time for that. Did Melvin have a girlfriend?"

"I think so."

"See how she is doing," he said.

What do you mean?" I asked.

"She may need a friendly face."

That thought was deep. It would have taken me some time to consider that. "I'll do it at his memorial services," I thought.

While riding I was hypnotized by the music and scenery, only to come out of my daze as Julius slowed to park.

"Where are we?" I asked.

"Hagerstown."

We entered the gate of an old Victorian style house, surrounded by a flower bed with rose buds starting to bloom in a well-manicured yard. A sign on the door read, "Mind and Body."

"Julius!" a woman's voice yelled excitedly. They exchanged the cordials and Julius introduced me and handed her a bag he got from the trunk. "I need the scales on it," he said.

The living room had about fifteen purple chairs and the walls were covered with pictures of beautiful scenes from nature. The coffee table was filled with Money, Sports Illustrated and Time magazines. I picked up the Money Magazine, but quickly put it back down.

The information inside did not register. Julius walked to the back with the lady, who looked Asian. The "Like Mozart" elevator music in the background convinced me that we were at his doctor's office. Men of different nationalities entered and exited, all of whom wore a shirt and tie. One of them who really caught my attention was sweating like Niagara Falls on legs.

A receptionist escorted me to another room and asked if I wanted a soda pop or water. The room was the same as the first with the chairs beautifully cushioned with oriental patterns. Relaxing music still flowed in the air. This room had a mirror measuring about a foot in height. It encircled the top of the wall all about.

The Asian woman who greeted Julius came in smiling and talking to someone behind the door, but I couldn't see who. She escorted me to Julius, who was sitting there with Larry.

"I heard you were knocking demons off shorty," Larry said sarcastically.

Julius chewing on an orange, said, "Yeah, my little youngin' had it rough today."

"We'll take care," the Asian woman said.

"I don't know. He's a little nutty," Larry said, "Hey, L, where is my money?"

"On my feet," I said.

The table held seven bricks of a white-yellowish substance, two one-gallon pickle jars with the smelliest stuff and an armor truck load of cash. *Oh my goodness, if Ant could see this*, I thought. The pursuit of happiness; goodness! A bottle of Remy Martin adorned the table while cigar smoke scented the air. Oh my goodness. The China babes made it picture-perfect.

"I told my peoples you had a bad day, so they gonna make it like Egypt for you. You the king, be a king." Julius said.

"How would you like that?" the Asian woman said.

"Cool." I nodded.

"I shouldn't have let you win my cash, Lil' Shorty," Larry said, disparagingly.

"Let?" I said. Larry had currency stacked to his knees. He didn't consider the fact that Ant and I played dice like the Romans. We played that game when our circle valued pennies. It wasn't an accident; it was our time.

"Yeah, let."

"Look at my feet. You paid for 'em," I said.

"My stack will drown you boy. Why y'all jump out

there?"

"We sit it down just like you."

"Ha. Right little L," the Mayor said. "He don't fool with your mess Larry."

"Shut up, Steve! Shut the hell up." Larry said, frustrated.

"Right, right, Larry," the Mayor said. "Way right, L is. Look, L. Look what I got." He pulled a bird from his pocket.

"Get that fuckin' dead bird out of here." Larry said.

"Steve don't worry about Larry. He's havin' a bad day. But why you got the bird in your pocket?" I asked.

"Man, look. A bad day? We got niggas asking about us, looking for us and you talkin' 'bout a bad day? Welcome to the inner city."

"Yo, don't be mad. If I catch you out there tonight, I'm gettin' another pair tomorrow," I assured him.

I had no fear of Larry. He looked weak and had always been on Ant and my chump list. I never disrespected him, but he had been getting in his feelings lately. He lost to us before, never on the semi-grand scale.

"What niggas are looking for you? I don't remember anyone saying someone was looking for Larry. So who is looking for you?" Julius asked.

"If they're looking for me, they are looking for you."

"You need to keep that shit out your mouth," Julius said.

"Hey cuz, I'm not trippin'." The door opened, and Asian woman was there with a young woman pointing in my direction, smiling. She motioned me over.

"Hey Larry, call me King L," I said.

"See? He talk too much," Larry said.

I followed her down some stairs and through two sets of doors to a room. The room had a chair, a bench and couch.

"What you name?" she asked.

I told her my name and she asked me to have a seat in the chair.

"Are you nervous?" she asked, as she began to massage my shoulders.

"Naw," I said, growling. That rubbing sure felt some kind of good. She used all her fingers, and at times used her knuckles while Tchaikovsky's "Theme from Swan Lake" played. Her hands moved with the cords on my shoulders, as if she was hitting notes on strings.

It had me static. I could not move. I was between peace and dreamland and hoping to stay there for a while. She asked me to take off my shirt and lay face down on the bench. The relief was refreshing as food rations to a war torn country.

Her kneading relieved stress and let life flow through my veins. Like butter on toast and olive oil on the head of our saints, the oils on the marble counter were good for my flesh, but also good for the internal as well.

Her touch relieved the stress Officer Thunderbutt had graciously given me.

She offered me tea and crackers. "Will relax you," she said.

"What's your name?" I asked.

"Mimi."

"I like this," I said, cheerfully.

"You Julius' brother?" she asked.

"No."

"Relax Larnell," she said, as I sipped the tea.

Relaxed I was, right into dreamland.

In dreamland, Peter Jennings was reporting about a menace named Mimi, who went around robbing police officers for their badges, sewing up their mouths and taking their pants. Then, I turned over and Brian Williams reported that she looked like a three hundred-pound Freddy Krueger, but she was as agile as an elephant.

Her face wasn't as burned. She wore no shoes, had no ears and only one toe per foot. A foot wide as Super Jack's pancakes, the toe was pointed upward and painted jade. Her clothes were made from animal hair and cotton cloth. She wore a cowboy's holster and her pistols were sterling silver. She got those made with the badges she took in the small towns.

Now the suspect was after the federal city police because of their solid gold badges.

"Mr. Williams, did she get Officer Thunderbutt?" I asked.

"I am sorry little urban soldier. There is no one by that name on the federal city police force," he said.

"Forgive me, sir, I mean Thunderbird," I said. "It's getting intimate. He's going to get it. Relief is coming and he's going to get it. Take his pants and sew him up," I thought.

"No, Officer Thunderbird is safe and sound!" Mr. Williams reported.

I woke up and I didn't know if it was because the female menace didn't catch the crooked cop or if it was the sound of a door shutting.

I was on my back, my nature was indurate and my pants were folded on the countertop. I thought to myself: "What was in the tea?" My body felt as light as a feather.

Steve rode back to the hood with Julius and me. "I am in love," I announced. "The next time you go here, let me know."

"You like the geisha, huh?"

"Oh yeah! I feel like I'm floatin' on clouds or somethin'."

The radio announced that two men were found dead in an apartment on Varney Street, Southeast. That was three blocks from our square.

"Varney? Damn!" Steve said.

"You all right little cuz?" Julius asked.

"Straight. I do have one question. What's in the tea?"

He laughed and said, "Relaxing herbs, baby."

"Two men, whose names have been withheld for further investigation, were shot execution style this evening.

Their hands and mouths were duct-taped. No drugs or money were found. If you have any clues or know something about this crime, please call the Wahington DC Police Department."

"Damn!" Julius said.

"Duct tape?" I said.

"Yeah, that's the war. This is war life. See, you duct 'em to shut 'em up. Valley Green was beefing with Fifteenth Place, but I know they ain't take it to this level. Hell no." Julius said as his mind began to wonder.

"Right, I heard all was cool," Steve said.

Julius' phone rang.

"Hey, little L, you got Larry's card, huh?" Steve asked.

"What happened around there?" Julius said to someone on the other end. "Yeah, I'm on my way," he paused. I know. I know, yeah. Damn! Has anybody seen him? He paused. "I'll be there in a minute."

"Fuck! It was Don Don's apartment," Julius said.

"Was it him?" Steve asked.

"They don't know, but Rock said he didn't think so."

En route, we drove past Don Don's place. The yellow homicide tape closed off the building to all family and friends. Police and emergency vehicles blocked the street with ringing lights. If you live in the building, you were locked in. Police knocked and then asked, "What you hear? What you see?"

And in most cases, nobody seen or heard a thing. We turned into the parking lot. Homies were sitting around, shaking their heads. Two of them ran up to the car and said, "Champ, it was Don Don's joint."

I always wondered whether this was normal living. A couple days ago my man Melvin lost his life. Now, four blocks away, two people were duct taped and shot in the heads. Hearing emergency vehicles every day was a part of my everyday, but it was a big, long jump to hood-law executions. Kind of reminded me of what I heard about Tombstone, USA. Is this possible? *Yes, and normal.*

Chapter

5

Our World

"Kack- kack- kack- kack." Automatic weapons thundered from a distance.

"That's a nine-millimeter," Rock said.

"It's probably a Mac 10," Steve rebutted. "That might be up Sixth Street or Third Street, huh?"

"Stop lunchin', Steve. That's in the Valley or up Wahler Place," Rock said.

Just imagine the reality. Training one's ear to decipher the sounds of gunfire. Their ears discerned an alto sax from a tenor sax, like a musician. Nines and Macs, I couldn't tell you the difference at that time if they were both put in my face, but I was learning. Steve and Rock were debating the time, distance and pop to determine the brand.

"Steve, go around Varney. Find out what's the deal," Julius said.

"Right. Let me get the bat?" the Mayor asked.

"What? You play baseball?" Julius asked.

"Julius, let me get my bat."

"No, I mean the Po-Pos are out there and two people have been shot in the head. And you want to carry a bat? No bat. You can't carry a stick to a gunfight."

"Fight?"

"Steve, do what I said."

Julius was in an agitated state and short on conversation. I was sitting on the porch contemplating whether or not I should ask him for some money to trim my pockets. I was trying to hit the ranking party later that night as well. The neighborhood was packed as speeding police cars and gunfire shared the atmosphere. People were talking about going up Cherry's. Cherry's served as a skating rink by day and a club by night.

Loitering and yapping, the hood's favorite pastime was in full effect. At least two dozen people moved around, killing grass and holding space on the concrete. Half of them surrounded Julius. It was Friday evening, the beginning of the Sabbath in ancient times, but in my hood, just a member of the world's daily mayhem. That weekend was lively. It was the weekend that celebrated Easter.

In the hood, families were serious about Easter. If you didn't go to church on any other day, you went on Easter, Black America's most cherished day on earth. Spirits were very high on Friday evening. It's the day people celebrate and worship to let loose of their problems. I took it all in as Ant walked up behind me spewing off frustration.

"Your name burns the loud speakers at school, you disappear, then Don Don's apartment gets blasted — but no sign of my nigga."

I turned and gave him hand dap, and said, "I got something to tell you."

"What up?" he asked.

"They got the cops on me."

"What!"

"Yeah. Nigga handcuffed me to Mr. Hawkins' chair. They tried to say I killed Melvin."

"You bullshittin'."

"I wish. But forget that. Man, Julius took me to a spot where the girls look like movie stars. They rubbed a nigga down and made me feel like a feather and the money was thicker than a thirty-eight inch snow storm. Nigga's cash was thick. Know what I'm sayin'?"

"They handcuffed you?"

"Yeah. I wanted to ask Julius for some money, but that Don Don stuff got his mind warped."

"What the police officer say?"

"He'll lock me up for spitting, and he'll see me soon."

"Damn. For real?!"

"Yeah, but forget that bum. But out Hagerstown, kid," I said, "Julius had these China babes giving me the royal treatment!"

"For real?"

"Yo, over the top."

"You going out?" Ant asked.

"Got to," I responded.

"You gotta talk to big cuz? Ant said.

"Later."

Ant and I left the counselors to counsel Julius. We went to suit up for the ranking party. Ant advertised a pair of New Balance, Levi's 550 blue jeans and a HOBO tee shirt. I had on an all white t-shirt, a pair of Calvin Klein painter jeans and you know it, my Top Ten red-striped Adidas.

"Ronald should be at the corner store," Ant said.

"Who at Cherry's tonight?" I asked.

"Rare Essence, Experience Unlimited (EU) and The Junk Yard Band," Ant said.

We scooped Ronald and paid the cover. Moe and the Junk Yard Band had just finished. The DJ was playing cuts from Notorious B.I.G, Sade's *"Love Deluxe"*, and Trouble Funk's, "Trouble" single. The scene was live with laughter and mingling all about.

"What happened to you today?" Ronald asked.

"Your principal," I said.

"Huh?"

"Don't worry about it. I'll tell you later."

Live music, the amps, the watts and the penetrating vibrations from the giant speakers took me somewhere else. The news reported it as jungle music. They said it called the African heart to fight, where the people have no control and chaos is the climax. I went to hear the bands put it in the pocket. We called it the socket. That's when the musicians played and they played to the rhythm of dance, no voice, just music. I loved that.

"What happened?" Ronald asked.

"I saw the other side," I answered.

"Hey, hey girl. You looking good in those spandex," Ronald said.

"Yeah, mama," I seconded that motion.

Sound man was testing the drums as they echoed off the walls, with the boom tap, boom boom, tap.

The bass guitar shook the nerves and the Congo drum, yes, the Congo talked to our hearts. This instinctive music called Go-Go was not graded by a bar. It came from Africa, through Sir Duke Ellington and then in line by Sir Godfather Chuck Brown. The record companies said they don't know how to market the music. That's because they don't understand our music.

Washington, D.C. is the home of Duke Ellington, the man who brought the jungle to Harlem. Like the song "Jungle Nights In Harlem" you could hear the seeds of Go-Go. Take even the song "Ko-Ko," though I wouldn't say we took the K and replaced it with the G. If you add jazz instruments and the instruments from the cover of Duke's "A Drum Is a Woman," there is the music they call Go-Go.

Chuck Brown's, "It Don't Mean a Thing (If It Don't Have the Go Go Swing)." We remember from Sir Ellington's, "It Don't Mean a Thing (If It Ain't Got That

Swing)." A massive coincidence, but when you add Curtis Mayfield and James Brown in the mix, the sum is Go-Go.

The band EU was playing *"Da Butt"* while we watched the gambling in the bathroom. Light green walls with graffiti and other writings announced street captains and gangs. Ant set a bet for thirty dollars and left with sixty. By the time Rare Essence came on the set, we were on the floor.

"..The teasingest torso tossing yet, and how!" The *Variety* reporter stated, of the women dancers who performed from music arranged by Duke Ellington at the Cotton Club, and they tossed and tossed. I don't know what it was, but the music had the women touching the floor and moving to the imagination of penetration.

The Mic Controllers (MCs), Jas. Funk and Lil' Benny conducted Rare Essence like Duke Ellington and Count Basie did their orchestras with cues, gestures and a lot of practice.

The spotlight flashed in and out while DJ Storman Norman handed the boards over to the band. Lava party lamps set in the black painted windows. Mirrors covered the walls like wall paper in a kitchen. And the overhead disco ball spun around and around.

"Man, you need to roll your pants legs down," Ant told Ronald.

"For what? You don't like my socks?" Ronald asked.

"Why do you have both pants legs rolled up? I mean your socks don't even match, man?"

"They do. They match my hat," Ronald said.

He had a tan apple jack hat, a yellow shirt, blue jeans, tan socks and some blue suede Nikes. He messed up my whole equilibrium. I felt psychedelic just standing by him. I didn't know if it was the tan hat or the blue shoes, and then, on top of that he had both pant legs rolled up.

"Hey, L!" The MC shouted, "is that you, baby?" As we moved closer to the front, I put my hands up to let it be known.

"We got L, Ant and the Sons of Caesar," the MC continued. "Say what now? They come to boogie with y'all."

We had our hands up, swinging and rocking while the band hit a pocket.

I started to move through the crowd with the hope that I'd get away from Ronald. The women were dancing in trances that induced me to get up on them, closer and closer. It only seemed natural as the band hit a peak.

"I knew it, I knew it, look Larnell," Ant said.

I looked and it was the young lady I met at the store. She was in a deep hypnosis. The music had her.

"That's it. I saw her here," Ant said.

"Hey," I said as I moved behind her. She kept moving and moving. I put my hands on her hips and she just moved. I said, "I knew it." She said nothing, but moved like a gypsy before the king.

"You didn't call?" I said, as I moved closer. She moved her braids to the side and smiled.

"Hey, White Boy, give them the stings and… Lets "Do The Mickey" say, Go-Go Mickey,'" Jas. Funk chanted.

Ronald came by my side doing the Running Man dance, moving back and forth like he was really running.

Ant stood there rocking the dome. A party train line came through deep, about fourteen dudes in it. The head of the line stopped in front of Kim. He got so close I could smell his breath. Kim laughed, and I swear I thought he called us bums.

"That's your friend?" I asked.

"Yeah," she said.

"Turn around," I said. She turned and seduced me with her eyelids. "Am I your friend?" I asked.

"Not yet," she answered.

"I think that just changed," I said as I pulled her close and rubbed my cheek against hers. I wanted to see if she smelled like roses.

"Hey, lover boy, they cranking like shit!" Ant said.

Yeah, she sure is, I thought and nodded.

The Go-Go train came back our way again with Kim's friend at the head. He stopped in front of us and stared. "What's up?" I asked. Without saying a word he started the train again and stepped on my Top Tens as he passed. "What! I'll tell you right now, you're knocking at the wrong door," I said.

"What up?" Ant asked.

"Calm down. He didn't mean it," Kim said.

"What's his name?" I asked, as he disappeared through the crowd.

"Yeah!" The MC said, "Valley Green is here."

"What you mean, calm down? Look, look at my shoes. I didn't buy them to be stepped on anytime your friend feels like it."

"They're all right, but who did it? Was it the short dude in the front?" Ant asked.

"Not today, yo!, Not my top tens, what!" I said, looking around in disgust.

Ronald slid by doing a break dance move. "What's up, yo?" he asked, as he did Michael Jackson's moon walk.

"A dude stepped on his shoes," Ant said.

"Rock over there with two bad girls," Ronald said.

I didn't care who Rock had over there. You don't step on my tennis shoes. When you do, that's a matter of cold disrespect. He didn't even say excuse me or anything. I needed to find out who he thought I was.

"I'll be back," I told Kim. Gestured to Ant and we started to walk the floor.

"Was it the short dude?"

"Yeah."

We got to the front of the stage and the bodies were thick. Dudes were handing little notes to the MC's, so they could be called on display.

"Condon Terrace is here, Uptown, Uptown. They in the pit! Uptown, Uptown, in the pit! Hey L, we got Ant and the Sons of Caesar, do it!" The MC said.

We were noddin' our heads as we squeezed through.

"I don't see bamma," Ant said.

We walked back toward Kim in a little space and there he was in Kim's face again. I walked up to him expecting an apology. Instead of an apology, I got a solid blow to my jaw! It caused me to hit the canvas. Ant jumped after the dude with lunging blows. Trying to regain my balance, I was grabbed by the shirt and hit again and again.

Moving forward with chin down I threw uppercuts and hooks with some success. The crowd moved like dust in a windstorm. A piercing shot to my back caused me to blackout for a split second. Throwing hay-makers, I knew I had to break somebody's jaw. Screams and another blow to my jaw and that was the last thing I could remember.

Chapter

6

The
Other Side

I woke up to my mother's voice, "This is ridiculous," she said, as my eyes opened. "Look at you, on your back, huh, Mr. Tough Man? I know what. I'm going to send you to my brother."

Touching the tube in my arm, Ant said, "They stabbed you dog."

"Yo, look at your face. You should be in here too," I said.

"I ran into a few fists," he said laughing, "but I'm straight."

"You got one hundred and twenty stitches in your back. I am not going to watch my son die," my mother said.

"Mom, stop the madness, I'm ok."

"Get out of your dreamworld. You're on your back. The doctor said a couple more centimeters and you would've been on permanent rest."

"They got out on us, huh?" I asked.

"Did they?" Ant said. "If Rock and Ronald wouldn't have pulled us out of there, I don't know."

"What! Michael Jackson helped? Yo, what's up with Don Don?" I asked.

"Still on the run. Hey, Kim called about four o'clock this morning asking about you."

"For real?"

"Yeah. She gave Ronald her number for you."

"Where that bum at? Look, I told you, I'm goin' to get on her couch." While I was talking, Robin and her mother walked though the door and exchanged greetings with everyone.

"How are you?" her mother asked.

"Cool," I said, as I turned the television on.

"Do you hurt?" Robin asked.

"My jaw," I said. She handed me some candy and a get well card.

"Where you coming from?" I asked.

"Church."

"On a Saturday?"

"What difference does that make? She's here," my mother said, looking at the lady in the other bed.

"I was…"

"You wasn't saying nothing. You know nothing. Robin, take my son to church. Can you do that for me?"

"Yes, ma'am."

"Hey, Ant," Robin said, "I guess you were fighting too?"

"You could say that," he said, mugging.

"Where were you fighting?" Robin's mother asked.

"At a party," Ant answered.

Robin gave me a repulsive look when Ant said that and I knew why. I told her I wasn't going to Go-Go's for a minute.

Robin's complexion was Sahara desert brown and her hair was red off the sun's rays. When I first saw her, it was like she was the sun's glory. She walked like she was Elizabeth I, a real queen of queens. Her habits were refined like she was bred for a loyal courtship. She made me wait four months for a kiss, unheard of in the hood.

"Y'all need to be careful out there," Robin's mother said.

"I don't know," Robin said, shaking her head.

"What's that baby?" My mother asked.

"I don't know," she said, and began to swell. Robin and I have been friends for about a year and a half.

"You shouldn't hurt her," my mother said. The woman in the other bed was an older white lady, who kept saying Happy Easter! "She really cares about you," my mother continued.

Too serious if you ask me, I thought. I shook my head and said, "I know." As the sun was ending its run for the day, my visitors slowly left. "Julius, Rock and Larry came to the hospital last night, but you were out on your back," Ant uttered.

"Word?"

"Word is bond. He asked me what happened and I told him. We couldn't do nothing, they were too deep for us."

"Yeah, I don't know why we even thought we could," I said.

"You," Ant said.

"Me? You the one talking about knocking somebody out," I said.

"They didn't step on my shoes, remember that, huh!"

"Happy Easter! Young men, be careful, you come too far to die over small matters," my roommate said. Ant looked at me and I at him.

"What the white lady talkin' bout," Ant whispered.

I shrugged..

"It's a disgrace," my roommate said, as she opened the curtains.

"Your name is Larnell?" she asked.

"Yes, ma'am."

"And your name is Anthony?"

"No, they call me Ant."

"Your parents named you Ant?"

"No."

"How old are you guys?"

"We're both sixteen," I said.

"You got your whole life ahead of you. But you're not going to see it, if you don't look over and beyond. Over and beyond, Happy Easter."

"Oh, boy," Ant sighed.

"How do you go through so much? Why, you don't even know half the story, do you? Happy Easter. Thank you Lord."

I had no idea what the lady was talking about; how we go through so much; the story.

"What story?" Ant asked.

"It's a disgrace."

"Good afternoon, Mrs. Edwards," the nurse interrupted, as she entered our room, speaking over the sound of the television and our voices.

"Humph. It won't be a good afternoon 'til I smoke me a cigarette," Mrs. Edwards said slowly.

"The doctor is about to sign your discharge papers," the nurse said.

"Good."

"Yes, it is good, but you're going to have to change some habits, like smoking."

"Fine time to tell me to stop smoking. Did I tell you Happy Easter?!"

"Yes, Mrs. Edwards. Not only are you to stop smoking, you should modify your diet as well. This means less ham, salty meats and oils. You've been diagnosed as having angina," the nurse said, closing the curtain.

Fighting for air was the voice of the news reporter on TV as he recapped that the big story of the day was the dress. "It has been leaked that, if they find the dress, they will find President Clinton's DNA."

"What? They trying to say the president is gay now?" Ant questioned.

The evening news continued. Kenneth Starr's office believes that the story of Betty Currie has the potential to do the greatest damage."

"Kenneth Starr is a sex crazed man," Mrs. Edwards said. "A sex crazed man."

Mrs. Edwards was a medium built woman with sandy-red hair. She had reached the golden age where watching what you say is not more important than being heard. She has seen and experienced some of those roads Ant and myself had yet to travel.

"All because of sex," I said.

"They're trying to get President Clinton out the White House because he likes black people, and now they're looking for a dress," Ant said.

"Who told you that?" I asked. "It's a lot of stuff going on, but the dress belongs to the lady. They say she wore it when she polished his knob. They say he left some protein on it," I said discretely.

"That's what everybody is saying, huh?" Ant asked.

"I don't know what everybody is saying. Do you look at the news?"

"News don't tell you nothin' but lies."

"Boy, you crazy," I said, as Julius, Rock and Steve walked in the room. Steve was behind the lot, laughing as he entered the room.

"Hey, L," Steve said, "I caught that bum Larry, right, talking about he like being on his knees."

"Word?"

"Right. Think he's trying to be like Ms. Lewinsky, huh L? Huh?" Steve asked.

"What's up little cuz?" Julius asked, laughing and handing me a bag.

"Trying to get out this joint," I said.

"Don't rush it. A little rest don't hurt," he said, giving Ant some dap.

"What's up sidekick?" he asked Ant.

"Trying to be like you, big dog." Ant answered.

"Do we got beef?" Julius asked, looking at me. "Do you know who done this shit?"

"Not really. Me and Ant got it, though."

"You ain't got nothing. You'll be on your back for a good minute," Rock said.

"You and Ant got what?" Julius asked.

"It was just a rumble," I said, as I opened the Footlocker bag Julius gave me. I pulled out a HOBO t-shirt and another pair of Top Ten Adidas. The same color I just bought. The same pair I had on last night.

"I thought you could use another pair kid, too much blood on the other ones. It didn't look like just a rumble last night. It look like someone wanted to hurt you."

"They did hurt me, but where them other joints at?" I asked curiously.

"Your moms got 'em."

"L, they were trying to kill you." Rock said.

"Well, they didn't."

"Sometimes it's blood for blood. You'll realize that soon enough."

"I'm trying to realize some money, you know, a little cake? That's the way. I'm trying to go about it. Them dudes are gonna get it, one way or another. But right now I am focusing my energy on making some paper, and we need you to get on man." I said, pointing at Julius.

"We'll have time to talk," he said.

"You're moving on now," the mayor said.

"This is how it feels to move on?"

"Right," Julius said. "He will talk, right?" the mayor said.

I found myself staring at the ceiling after they left. Yellow and blue butterflies control the ceiling of the weak and weary. Tubes and liquid bags supported my flesh to life. All I thought about was getting out of the hospital and talking to Julius. Thinking, at last, my just due was coming. It's our time to get our issue.

Julius is going to hook us up. I know this. I know this. I'll make sure we get "Paid in Full." I'll make sure I hook my mother up and stack some cash for a rainy day. I'll make sure the money work itself and we'll stay paid. We won't have to take Jimmy Dean sausages anymore for Ms. Parker, who owe us about twenty dollars.

"She is a lovely young lady," Mrs. Edwards said, putting an end to my lucrative daydream. Is that an older people thing or something? She just started talking.

"Have you ever heard of Bessie Coleman?" she asked. I said, "naw," but thought she could have been some kin to the star of *Different Stokes*.

"You know, she really likes you," she said, as the nurse entered our room.

The nurse told me due to my fever she had to administer an antibiotic. She said, "Fevers are signs of an infection." She also told Mrs. Edwards to, "Remember that fatty meats and smoking is clearly the worst thing you could do."

"I've been smoking for forty-six years and no doctor is going to tell me to stop," Mrs. Edwards said.

"Less ham, salty meats and oils as well," the nurse said.

"Ham!" Mrs. Edwards said, particularly upset that ham was not good for someone in her condition.

Good thing the nurse wasn't talking to my mother. She would have probably tried to choke the air out of her. For my mother, ham was a tradition, second only to turkey. It was not just the other white meat, but thee white meat. We had Thanksgiving ham, Christmas ham, and Easter ham. Ham was the offical holiday meat in my hood.

Mrs. Edwards told the nurse that ham had kept her and her husband alive after they had been chased out of Macon, Georgia, for their interracial love-making. "It seemed like the 'Underground Railroad,'" she said. "We traveled about thirty-five miles door to door, until we reached Atlanta. And guess what? We purchased two pigs that kept us alive until we reached the north.

"Mrs. Edwards, I'm accustomed to eating pork myself, but these are instructions from your doctor."

"My family wanted to kill him, you know?" Mrs. Edwards said.

"Sorry to hear that."

"Good evening," the television announcer interrupted with a news bulletin. "The police have confirmed to News Four that they have in custody the man responsible for two of the three murders last night in Southeast Washington." *Damn, they got Don Don*, I thought. *Julius didn't seem sad or distracted today.*

On the TV screen appeared, a young black man, a menace to society, with his head down, an assumed position since slavery.

I picked up the phone but heard no dial tone. "Hello? Hello?" I said.

"Hello," the voice returned.

"Who is this?" I asked.

"Kim."

"Oh, the reason I lay on my back, huh?"

"How are you doing," she asked.

"Well, they freakin' say I got a fever. My man told me you called."

"Your man is crazy, talkin' 'bout what he gonna do to people. I didn't have nothing to do with what happened."

"You need to control your boyfriend. Shit like this could get out of control," I said.

"That's not my boyfriend."

"He shouldn't have jumped out there like that."

"I was crying," she said sentimentally.

"Don't get mushy with me. You probably started crying when Ant was about to crack your head."

"He couldn't crack nothing but a Band-Aid box the way he looked." Why she say that about my man?

"Yeah, okay." I said.

"I called to say hi. I didn't call to talk about your friend."

"Hi," I said.

"When are you getting out the hospital?"

"You know, you didn't have time for me up Georgetown. What? It takes a nigga to get almost killed for some attention?"

"I didn't feel like talking to you."

"Me either," I said, as I hung the phone up. *Forget her*, I thought. *She's the reason I'm in the hospital anyway.*

A moment later my dial tone returned and I called Ant. He wasn't home, but I wasn't surprised.

I sat there watching TV, wondering whether or not that was Don Don I saw. The news was talking about the NCAA's March Madness tournament and Michael Jordan's sixth peat.

Michael Jordan was a modern day god. Forget him. That was three-fifths of a person turning into superman. How about a one man empire, an industry with a work ethic that mimicked that of Egypt.

While the TV continued to pound the local news, and of course President Clinton's problems, the phone rung.

"Yo, Ms. Parker is crazy, man." Ant said.

"I just called you."

"Yeah! Look, didn't we drop five and five on Ms. Parker, so she owe us twenty dollars, right." Before I could say a word, "Right," he continued. "Why she give me a two dollar bill, shut the door, and said that's it?"

"You should have asked her for the twenty."

"I did ask her for the dub. She said, 'that's it' or something like that."

"Oh, man, she got you. You suckerrrr. You let an old woman give you the moves," I said laughing.

"Naw, man. I think she is losing her mind, for real."

"Kim called me today. She told me you lunched out on her."

"Yeah, forget them dirty girls. But guess who I saw today?"

"Who?" I asked.

"Melvin's girl. She asked me about this watch and she said, the funeral..."

"Hello? hello?" I said. Ant didn't answer and there was no dial tone. *I know this bum didn't hang up on me*, I thought. Still no dial tone. I called the nurse. "Could you ask somebody to come to my room and fix the phone. It just cut me off," I said.

"It's time for the phones to turn off."

"Don't worry about them phones, they distract you," Mrs. Edwards said.

"What? You just turn the phones off just like that?"

"Yes, in this hospital the phones turn off at a certain time. Could I help you with something else?" The nurse asked.

"You got to be kidding. Not for real? They turn the phones off around here?" I said to myself. "These people are unbelievable. I got to get out of here."

"Yes, they do, but you could talk with me," Mrs. Edwards said, "You know Bessie Coleman was the first woman to receive an International pilot's license?"

I'll tell my sister, I thought. She talked about airplanes a lot.

"She was not allowed to attend 'an American flying school because of her race,' so she went to France to learn. If you really want something, you could have it," she said, "Like my husband got me and I him."

"So she was a black lady, huh?" I asked.

"Yes, she was."

"She went to France, huh?"

"Yes, and came back to America and died as she was thrown from her plane."

I was paralyzed to the real meaning behind Mrs. Edwards information. Melvin was killed a few days ago, Don Don had two dead bodies in his apartment and I'm in the hospital healing from ice pick gashes. Death has never been the same since my grandmother passed. But lately, it was an overdose, near critical condition. Julius and crew didn't mention anything about Don Don, so it couldn't have been him. And he didn't seem like the type to kill his own brother.

With that, the only things that really dominated my thoughts were money and how to stack it in piles. Call me narrow-minded, but the pursuit of happiness and gold was my objective. My cousin said he would talk with me. That was like the great gift wished for on birthdays. I couldn't ask for no more than that.

My mom and I took the taxi home from the care center. The taxi driver looked to be in his sixties. He was an African American who told her that he had served twenty-two years in the armed services. As the car entered Southeast, via South Capitol Street, he began to drive slowly, cautiously.

"I won't usually work here. Not me, homey," he said.

The word "homey" made my mother move her head back. "They're crazy," he continued. "It's not all of them, of course. It's only about ten percent of them. And, forgive me, but the women are just as crazy as the men."

"Hi, I'm Louise and you?" my mother said.

"I'm Ruppert," he said.

"Yeah, it's crazy out here," my mother said.

"They say, 'I'll be right back. You could hold my pocketbook. I'll be right back.' Huh, that's a big help. The young hoodlums hanging on the corner with their pants hanging down off their butts. They get in my car and talk about the white man this and the white man that. I tell them that the white man is not responsible for their problems.

They're responsible for their own problems. They're holding themselves down," he concluded.

"Do you have any children, sir?" I asked.

"No, I don't," he answered. None that he wanted to recall, I thought.

Shaking her head, my mother seemed to have concurred with some of what the cabbie was saying.

"Young people truly need some help. They can't do it all by themselves," she said.

"Ma'am, I agree, but they must help themselves."

"You know," my mother said, looking muddled. "I was watching the news the other night, and they reported that the CIA was responsible for bringing tons of cocaine into the U.S., now that's a government agency."

"I haven't heard that," he returned.

"Yeah, I saw a news report about five years ago on *60 Minutes*. Then the government, knowing this, started talking about one strike and you're out when caught with crack cocaine. Where's crack cocaine?" she asked. "In the inner-cities," she answered. "Now, I know many young people have died and been arrested because of that cocaine. Who do you blame?"

Man, my mother was jive serious. It was times like this that you knew she was captain Buck's daughter, when she talked about matters that didn't register as cause an effect. She had on those old polyester pants with the permanent crease. Her ways haven't changed much since the 1970s. She still presses her hair with a gas stove-heated hot comb.

The taxi driver simply shrugged as he approached our housing project. He didn't respond, but understood where she was coming from all the same.

Chapter 7

Mad Returns

"Did you take a bath when you were in there?" my sister asked.

"Naw," I said.

"See? I told you my brother is dirty. He didn't even take a bath," she said to her little friend as I sat on the porch in front of building 4200. She didn't have to stop cheerleading just to ask me that.

Southeast, Washington covers about a quarter of the Capitol city. It is known worldwide for its camps and inhabitants. The projects concentrated in this one area of the city aided its notorious reputation.

I sat there, still sore from last week's brush with death. Our hood is six miles from the nation's capitol building. You could see President Washington's monument on a hill from our hood. So close, yet so far away. The most important capitol in the world harbors some of the most dangerous hoods on earth.

No loitering signs labeled the red square monsters. I found myself there just looking about, thinking about Melvin and the fact that I missed his funeral.

Evening was coming over the set. Our hood had a permanent ice-cream truck sitting on bricks. It was the food mart on wheels.

It gave credit to the moneyless, took food stamps, and waited for the first of the month to collect some of those government handouts.

With all the broken glass and burnt cars stripped down to their frames, the community was rich with hard working mothers who took the A bus for their travels. They were the reason we felt so strong. From breast milk to Enfamil and produce from the local Safeway, they gave us strength to run this community and run it we did, as we saw fit. As I sat there watching some of them coming home from work looking exhausted with watermelon sized bags on their shoulders. I wondered about the fathers again. There was a boyfriend or two around but not a father.

Mothers of all sizes dominated our land with all their strength. Yet, it was not enough to stop the young, determined black male species.

"What up, champ? Hey, little soldier, and "God," they addressed me, when I came back to the set. You get elevated to another level when you beat death.

"Nigga!" Ant yelled, coming from the rear, "you back outside?"

"I'm back," I said, watching my cousin and Larry. Rock was across the yard talking to a woman, who couldn't stop moving and scratching. It was like every element of her body wanted attention. Signs of a crackhead.

"You ready, little cuz?" Julius said.

"Born ready."

"Come here," he said, gesturing me to follow.

We walked up the stairs in building 1000. The hallway smelled like a roll of port-a-johns. Permanent ink highlighted the walls with names of those who were there, some of whom have long since passed on. One read, "Meat

Top was here and now I am gone, I left my name to carry on, those who knew me very well those who didn't can go to hell." In the hood that's like art. The steps and hallway floors were of pure concrete. When you look back, you think about the mission behind project builders, "Get'em up."

The elevators never worked for me, but when they did work, you heard about someone getting hurt. It got to the point where I didn't think they were for riding. They reminded me of something from the Twilight Zone. The elevator was the toughest and most mysterious matter in that building. It was like you could disappear into another world just by entering it. The lime green center blocks gave base to the walls we painted with our pictures and thoughts.

This was my moment. Like a second interview, this was my moment to convince him and his doubts that I was ready. Little goose bumps hit me all over.

Maybe, I could move my mother out of Southeast and buy her a nice car or house, if it all goes well. All kinds of thoughts went through my brain about this possible promotion.

The apartment smelled like burnt foot powder as the TV blasted the movie *Apocalypse Now*. Steve was on his knees by the closet looking for something.

"What ya doin' Steve?" Julius asked.

"Did you see it? I know it was right there. Right there, right?"

"Steve, you were in the same position an hour ago. Is it that good?"

A futon couch sat on polished crème sedona Meridian Stone floors and a picture of Martin Luther King, Jr. decorated a wall in the living room. A 42-inch Sony color television sat beside a black 200-watt pioneer home entertainment unit. Steve was there crawling around like a hungry dog or something. "I know it's here," he said, as he crawled to the closet and went in.

"That's a crackhead." Julius said.

"Naw," I said, laughing. "He didn't just go in the closet like that."

"Yeah, he did. A'ight, what's up?" Julius said.

"What's up with Steve?" I asked.

"He's geeking," Julius said.

"Hey, Steve," I yelled.

"It's in here," he replied.

"What is he looking for?"

"Leave it alone, lil' cuz," Julius said.

"Me and my man need you, cuz," I said.

"You owe somebody or something?" he asked, with an incredulous look on his face.

"Naw," I said, "and we don't want to. I thought you could give us something to get on with."

"You trying to get my aunt to kill me?"

"Naw, she ain't got nothin' to do with this," I said.

"If you get caught doing the wrong thing. My name don't come up?"

"Julius, I ain't on that kind of time. Me and Ant tryin' to make some cash," I said.

"What you doing right now?" he asked.

"Shooting dice for it all," I said.

"Hmm. I got something for ya and I hate to see ya go outside the circle. If you want to hustle," he said, "the first thing you need to know is that it's just that, a hustle. It's not value for value. It's a scheme and a scam with a few up-rights in between on every corner. You got that! Don't fuck with crack, shit is too hot. I mean it, Lil' L. It's getting us paid but the drama is crazy. You'll start with Lovely, but where you end, now listen and watch, because where you end, I can't promise."

"I know," I said.

"Know this lil' cuz," he continued. "This game don't have many lifers. We don't have medical plans and shit like that. Don't fuckin' think, you could do this forever."

"I'm trying to get it like you," I said.

"You want to be like me, and I 'want to be like Mike.' Look, you get your grind and roll. Like me, I am making moves and I am trying to roll, soon. I think a little production company is that move."

He poured a half gallon of orange juice and thirteen bottles of vanilla extract in the sink. Washed out the bottles and pulled out a quarter pound of hemp from a gym bag full of drug paraphernalia, including heavy duty aluminum foil, silicone plastic paper and zip-lock storage bags. He then showed me how to chop the weed and mix it with one ounce of liquid that looked like Mountain Dew.

The liquid had an alluring and distinctive smell like pickle juice and Clorox bleach. He shook the mixture up in the empty orange juice bottle. He took the liquid in the pickle jar and funneled it at one ounce increments in all thirteen of those vanilla extract bottles. It looked like the same jar I saw on the table out Hagerstown.

"Each bottle costs three hundred dollars," he said, looking directly in my eyes.

This is my hood's most viable method to advance economically. With my cousin as a guide, financial success seemed within easy reach. PCP (Phencyclidine, Lovely, Green, Angel Dust, Love Boat) was my ticket to money-making and, therefore, to what I believed was true happiness.

Any consideration of whether this happiness would last never crossed my mind. But it was on my cousin's mind. The scope of my vision was minute, so minute, in fact, that Congress Heights seemed to have all the resources that I thought I wanted and needed.

My goal was to be content, and from my perspective, the pursuit of happiness meant the pursuit of wealth.

He measured the mixture on a baby spoon and poured it

onto small aluminum foil squares and folded the squares into little boats. He told me each boat would cost fifteen dollars. "They called sacks," he said. And three hours later I had more than one hundred little sacks. "Create a demand. Give a few away and give Steve some, he'll point you out. I'm charging you one hundred and fifty for each bottle. It's three hundred outside of us. You got that?" he asked. "I'm not dealing with nobody but you. Not even your man out there. You deal with your man, and trust no one."

I was set. Made. Dreams do come true. I stuffed them all in a zip-lock bag and into my pants.

"You don't want to do that just yet, know what I am saying?" he said. "That's too much. You got bills and I want my money. Take twenty to forty outside and leave the rest in the freezer."

"Can I do it my way?" I asked.

"No, you can't. Take fifty and leave the rest in the freezer and take this key to get back in," he said, like a foreman would to his construction crew.

The block was still jumping and my man Ant was still there. He hugged and kissed me when I showed him the goods. "Fuck yeah!" He said.

I gave Ant twenty sacks to pad his loins. "Come here," I said, as we walked to the playground.

I ran through the whole spiel. "I knew he was going to hook us up," Ant said.

The night was clear. Seventy degrees of sweet spring air.

Springtime, smiles, love and money. I saw this very well. I looked to the heavens and took a deep breath of fresh air. *I can't believe it*, I thought. I was excited as if I had just received a green card or won a million dollars in the D.C. lottery's Powerball.

Ant moved back and forth shouting, "Lovely." I grabbed the broken chain hanging from the swing's supporting cross bar.

Ant sat on the only working swing and tied his Tims. I felt like we grew a hundred inches with those sacks in hand, like every breath gave an increase.

"Lovely," we yelled, over and over.

"Lil' L, right there. Two coming at you, right," Steve said, pointing at two people coming our way.

"Lovely," I said.

"Yeah, can I see?" the woman asked.

I handed her a sack. "We got that. That's right, we got that," Ant sung. She put it up to her nose and asked for another.

"It smells good," she said. She was a thin woman with blue jeans, a black Members Only wind breaker and had a pair of dusty Nikes on.

"Give me three," she asked, pulling out a hundred dollar bill.

"Damn, I don't have change for that."

"That's all right I'll come back," she said.

"Naw, we goin' get change for ya," Ant said, running off to the circle. "This is that thing. You hear me? That thing they been talking about." I continued the sale.

The Mayor directed traffic our way and we sold our product like the clerks in Nordstrom's fragrance department. Old and young were buying our 'Green'. The one thing they had in common was - each one of them sniffed the sacks before purchasing.

"How you feeling?" Ant asked.

"Sore."

"How many more do you have?" he asked.

"Not many. How about you?" I asked.

"Two."

The broken playground unit sat behind the circle. From our position near the swing the circle and the parking lot, were in good view. I felt fatigue as the night wore on. Sitting on the sliding board, I continued, "We got that Lovely, yeah, that thing they been talking about," I advertised. The playground had about thirteen people holding space. "Lovely," I said.

"Look at this man," Ant said, as he pulled out pockets full of cash.

"Y'all doing all right?" Steve asked.

"More than that. Look at my man," I answered.

"Put your money up. Here comes two more. You looking?" Steve asked.

"Yeah," Ant said, pulling out the money again.

"You don't want to do that out here," Steve said.

"Look at this. Hey L, we never had it like this. I hear you Steve, but ain't nobody going to take this from me. I've been waiting too long. Tell him, L. I'd like to find someone who wants to drop some tonight."

"Naw, man. We ain't doing that tonight. Business first. We got bills off of this."

"You said we have a rack of this stuff."

"Man, we got bills," I said, as we heard pitched voices in the circle. I thought about the stores, too, and which ones I was going to hit. But first things first. The money was due to big cuz and I wasn't going to treat it like a crap game purse o' how I wanted to. My soreness wasn't an issue as I looked around the yard. I felt like a Scrappa. *I am a hustler*, I thought.

Like selling Webster's dictionaries and Beringer's White Zinfandel, I finally got my product to sell and push. Yeah, to do it. I had to put it out there like, "I got that green. King of the green. Got that."

"Okay, Okay. Fuck that nigga!" Rock said. The group of loud voices moved toward the grounds. Julius was in the front telling Rock to cool it. Larry, Ronald, Wembo and Fingers walked around with three other guys.

"Oh, man. Shut the hell up. You lying fucker. Just step out of line one time," Rock yelled.

"Me no want no trouble," the Mag said.

"All right. Hold it. Hold it...."

"It's a better way to come," Larry said.

"Your name?" Julius asked.

Everything seemed urgent like debris flying in a tornado.

"Tony."

"You and your boys fuckin' come 'round here again like this," Larry said, chewing his lips.

"You just moved around, huh? Huh? Why you want to know me?" Julius asked.

"My cousin wanted to meet you," he said.

"Yea, mon," the alien said, "me Mag. I want to see if you could do something for us."

"What's that?"

"In private mon," Mag said.

"That's the same dude," Ant whispered.

"He just want to talk," one of those dudes uttered.

"What!" Rock said. "Talk about what?"

"Hey, yo, you wolfin'?" the stranger asked.

Two of those guys wore black pullovers. The dude Mag wore a full jumper and a down feather vest. The other dude had on a lumber jack shirt. Larry dressed in a yellow and black Versace shirt and black Phat Farm jeans. Rock had on a black navy pea coat, white tee shirt and tan shorts. His hands were in his pocket while standing beside Julius.

This scene was out of Tombstone when odds faced off. The rules were limited to our own interpretation. Dirt for yams was the thought considered. Blood on concrete was the sum to be interpreted.

"Yeah," Julius said.

"Oui," Mag said.

"That don't make no sense. Forget that shit," Rock said.

"Cool out Rock," Larry said.

"Wha he wolfin'!" the stranger said.

Larry looked at the stranger pulling his shirt up, saying, "No need for that," as his pearl handle showed.

"Man, niggas crazy, coming around like that," Ant said, with other voices more audible. I focused on Julius talking to Mag.

I couldn't hear them, but Julius looked curious with his fingers running through his goatee. Frontier politics, I thought.

Talk about one's interests under tension. The law allowed the rule of the jungle to stand with minimum interference. I watched Julius, admiring his every move. He looked ahead of the moment. He was in control of himself.

"I don't like him," Ant said, looking toward Julius and Mag.

"You don't even know him," I said.

"I don't have to."

In the apartment, Ant and I unloaded about twelve hundred dollars of that "mean green" on the bed in the second room. The room was laid out with contemporary oak head and foot boards. It had two matching dressers and an armoire. The window draperies were black with gray and black diamonds. Ant's eyes were sparkling at the sight of freedom's paper.

"Man, we could've bet this loot. I know somebody in there tryin' to drop some," Ant said.

"It don't matter. We got bills."

"What we owe? I been out there, too. I get someone?"

"We owe $1,850. Yeah, you been out there? You startin' to trip already? I'm going to give you a hundred and after we pay these bills we'll drop whatever," I said.

I wasn't interested in spending before we paid Julius. The money looked good, but it didn't look that good.

"A hundred dollars?" Ant asked.

"Here you go, drop them! You need to learn how to hold on to money." I said.

Two knocks and then she entered the room. She was the same woman who passed Ant and I while we were on the playground. With her head down, she went straight to the closet and then he opened his mouth.

"I'm goin' in tomorrow."

I just put my head down and looked perplexingly toward Ant. Inside I was laughing. Don Don fooled the crap out of me. When he took off the wig, I was stuck. I could not get one word out my mouth.

"Oh, shit! That's gangster," Ant shouted. "Man, you dress like a girl?" He had on blue knickerbockers and a white and blue shirt with a pink sweater. What extremes would you go to in order to preserve your freedom? He had on a pink sweater! Ant thought it was gangster. But I thought it was serious, yet funny.

He was wanted by the police, but for him to dress like a woman made me wonder. Looking at him, I cleared my throat, and said, "I'm goin' to drop this nine hundred with Julius."

"Why you looking like that, L?" he asked, in a calm voice. "You goin' give him all that?" Ant asked.

I just looked at him.

"Hey, "L." What's up? You wanna call the police?" Don Don said.

"Naw, you don't believe that," I responded. "You just got me confused."

"I might turn myself in tomorrow," he said.

"Yeah?"

"Man, why you wanna do somethin' like that?" Ant asked.

"I ain't running from them peoples. I needed to make sure shit was in order. Fuck 'em. They don't have shit on me!"

I wanted to ask did he do it, but it wasn't my business so I left it alone. I just made the most money I had ever made and beside me was a guy who was accused of killing his own brother.

My real concern was my finances, getting Julius this nine hundred and getting back on the block right away. I gave Steve fifty for the lookout. I felt like time had come, and I thought it wasn't by chance numbers were starting to roll in.

Julius, Larry, Rock and Jumbo sat at the dining room table with dominos scattered about like marbles at a thumb shootout.

"Larry, what's up?" Ant said, shaking the dice.

"I ain't chasin' your little money, shorty. Keep your pennies," Larry said.

"Little money? What's that?" Ant asked.

Steve was sitting in the living room, laughing out of his mind. "Man look at this nigga," Steve said, excitedly, about Colonel Kilgore (played by Robert Duvall).

"He was givin' water to a dying Vietcong, right," he continued, "and a dude told him, a surfer was there, right? He just threw the damn water away!"

"Steve, how many times you goin' to watch that?" Julius asked.

"Forever," Steve said, sipping on an Old English 800. I sat on the futon to see what Steve's thrill was all about.

"He's crazy," Steve kept repeating, as Col. Kilgore was playing the guitar. Steve explained that *Apocalypse Now* was about Vietnam and that it was the best movie ever made.

"Dag, is that Laurence Fishburne?" I asked.

"Yeah, he looks like he's about twelve, huh?"

He did look baby-faced, but not twelve. My uncle said once that Vietnam was the Black man's sacrifice to honor and employment.

With the surround sound bouncing audio off the walls and my interest in history, the movie really came to life. Lieutenant Willard (played by Martin Sheen) was traveling by boat with a crew. He had orders to "seek out a renegade" and "terminate with extreme prejudice." He needed Colonel Kilgore, and his air cavalry to transport them over land. This cavalry replaced the old world horse mounted cavalry. By air, they traveled and fought to dismount.

"See what I am saying, right? All he thinkin' 'bout is surfin'." The Mayor said.

"Domino!" Julius yelled.

"Wembo, yous a stupid motherfucker. You saw him playing threes; you let him keep the whole. Man, let me sit there and you holding the three-duce. Why you didn't play it? You big stupid. I mean, in the mirror, you and stupid look the same," Larry said.

"I play my hand and you play your hand," Wembo said.

"That's right. Forget that faggot, Wembo," Don Don said.

"But you came in here with a pink sweater," Larry said.

"Man, wash them dishes ya faggot," Don Don said.

"Hey," Julius said, "I need you to get one for Mag and I want $18,000 up front."

"Look! Look L, check it out," Steve said.

They mounted to the sound of the bugle and over the sparkling blue water and in the sun's sight. The air cavalry's silhouette came to Vinh Dinh Drap. The Col. had the "Ride of the Valkyries" blasting from mounted speakers on the helicopter. He said, "The sounds of Wagner scared the slopes."

They flew right into battle. Helicopters were falling. Bombs were blowing up bridges. Enemy fire was piercing and bouncing off the helicopters armor and the Col. was excited about the waves.

"Look at him," Larry said, laughing. The Col. was definitely a little crazy. All he kept saying was, "The waves, the waves" when bullets were flying all around.

I heard my uncles talk about Vietnam, but I don't recall them telling me about anyone like Col. Kilgore. Col.

Kilgore's mission was to get them to Vinh Dinh Drap and that he did, even if the six-foot swells were what excited him most. Steve fell to the floor, laughing and choking on his own drool. Tears even came down his face.

"Crackhead, that shit ain't that funny," Larry said.

"Larry, let me crack your head," Ant said, shaking the dice.

"If you're dropping $500, give me five minutes," he said, in a high voice, while smacking the table with the bone. I left Steve and his drooling on the futon. The dominoe game got very loud. They were smacking the table as hard as a major league bat hit a ball.

Wembo was very quiet and didn't say much. I don't think he ever started a conversation with me. Him and Rock were different people. Wembo was about 6 feet tall and I thought he always had stories in his head. I would catch him from a distance just laughing to himself. When I would speak, he'd just say, "Cool."

I sat there and watched them play and talk. They were taunting each other, trying to expose weaknesses.

Larry took the game very serious, insulting Wembo at every turn. Wembo shook his head or said, "I play mines and you play yours," in his deep voice.

"Damn, you got it," Ant yelled. "I let Steve get me."

"Right, right. What? You want some?" Steve asked me.

"I ain't messin' with you."

The conversations, as the time went on, began to deal with the business. Long after my man Ant went home, Julius told Don Don that on the legal front he had everything in order.

Rock mentioned that he didn't like Mag's approach and that something was not right.

"We'll watch that, but right now, let's see how much business we could get from the jake." Julius said, lighting a cigar.

"Something's up with that," Rock repeated.

"We will see. I talked with Gab over at 93 WKYS and it looks like we'll get more then a few tickets for their Hip-Hop/Go-Go party next month."

"Good," Larry said.

"Whatever we want, our contract is $20,000 over four months. We move this business to real business and I think this might be it. We got to find a way out and I think a production is the way," Julius said.

"And then what? It ain't goin' bring cake like the streets. Champ I don't think it's a good ideal," Rock said.

"We gonna flip this shit to a store or something," Julius answered.

"I hope I'm out before that. It was self-defense this time," Don Don said.

Walking home, I wondered whether Don Don meant he had killed his brother in self-defense. I thought I would ask Julius sometime later, but I knew one thing, Ant and I were going to that WKYS party. *I could see it now*, I thought, *women everywhere.*

Chapter

8

Master
Douglass

"Keep it up. You hear? Just keep it up. I got something for you," my mother said, while I was going to my room.

"Do what, mom?"

"You feeling better now, huh? I didn't ask you to do a damn thing."

"Huh?"

"Oh, no, you must be feeling better, coming in here this time at night."

I told myself not to say a word. I kept repeating to myself, "Don't say a word. Don't say a word

"Keep it up. Oh, you feel better, you think you grown?"

"Mom, what I do?"

"Got damn it, just keep it up!" she said, slamming her bedroom door.

She was bugging out. She was probably still upset about me fighting. My heart was bubbling with happiness as I was lying down to sleep. My man Ant and I got some currency flow. Julius looked out real big. Back to school tomorrow. Didn't really feel like it, but mom insisted. The ceiling disappeared as the good thoughts of the day went by.

The phone rang as dreamland was taking hold.

"What up?" I answered, sluggishly.

"Hi, what you doing?" Kim asked. What did she think I was doing at 2:30 in the morning?

"Nothin'."

"I was just checking on you," she said.

"I'm straight. How you doin'?" Inside I was happy; I wanted to talk to her. She was the prettiest girl I had ever seen, besides my Robin. I wanted to sit on her couch for real.

"Can I ask you a question?" I asked, "And I ain't trying to be funny or anything, but do you have a couch?"

"A couch?" she inquired.

"Uh, yeah. I got this thing with couches and thought it would be nice if we could sit on it and talk, since I don't have your number."

"Boy you crazy," she said, laughing.

"That's what they say."

"I think they right. How is your friend?"

"Straight. I'm tryin' to come and see you."

"Do you got a beeper or a phone?" she asked.

Now, I got to have a beepa or a phone to get with her, I thought. *First thing tomorrow I'm going to get one.*

"Naw, your boy's crew took it. I'll get another one tomorrow," I answered. What else was I supposed to say?

"What? They took your phone and a beeper. You had both?"

"Naw, don't worry about it. I'll give you a number to reach me. So, when can we hook up?"

I really wanted to see her again. She was like Nefertiti, straight had it going on. Her lips were perfect, not too big and not too small, just beautiful and full. When we danced together at the party, I felt something special and I hope she did too. She was in the top twenty best looking in the city. Yeah, she was like that.

"You got a girlfriend?" she asked.

"I like that dance you gave me at the party," I said.

"You can't answer me?"

"Naw, I'm just tired. That dance you gave me, yeah that was nice. I don't have a girlfriend. I have friends but not like you; Mrs. I got enough male friends. Remember you said that at the store?"

She gave me her number and told me she lived on Wheeler Road, Southeast and that she went to Dunbar Senior High School. She lived with her grandmother, and I was sure she had a couch because grandmothers always had couches and coffee tables.

She told me the guy I was fighting was an old boyfriend and that she was sorry that it had happened, because she was having fun with me. We talked about hooking up in a few days. I couldn't make any promises as Ant and I had business. My heart opened like a flood gate, pumped up and in a rush it went, pumped up; and I liked the feeling.

My mother couldn't wait to wake me up for school. "Get up, get up. If you can go outside, you can go to school." She couldn't wait! "Did you fill out that application for CVS?"

"Yeah," I said.

"Where is it."

"I already took it back," I said, as my little sister stood there shaking her head, looking at me and talking about, "No you didn't."

"Shut up!"

"Mom, he didn't take it back. He's lying."

"Pooh, did I ask you? Get yourself ready," my mother said. Little sisters should be outlawed. As I got myself pepped up off the smell of mom's coffee, granddad walked in. He had two books in his hand and asked me whether or not I finished the other books yet.

Granddad had on a pair of dandelion slacks, an apricot-colored button-up shirt with stripes and a pair of red socks. His slacks were high waters, with winged Stacy Adams. *How could he do it?*

"I'm almost finish."

"I'm almost. Boy, this world wasn't almost. I almost had a job. I almost. It ain't no joke out there, I've been in World War II and my sons been in Vietnam. Just because you have some scratches on your back means nothing," he said, looking like he had a drink or two.

"I'm a finish." I said.

"I almost. I got another one for you, listen to this."

"Dad, he needs to get ready," my mother said.

"No, baby, he needs to know these things. Now Frederick Douglass lived right here in Southeast, Washington, D.C., right here, a few blocks up the street. He was born into slavery in 1817, escaped to the North, and became the greatest leader-spokesman for the blacks of his era.' Now, listen Larnell. Listen to this."

Granddad was so serious. I guess he heard my mother slamming the door. He had given me books since I was in the ninth grade, so I knew he took books very personal. He was a drinker but a wise man.

I think it was his duty in World War II, and the fact that he read so many books that made him so eager to have his children and his children's children stay focused. I think he was the reason I was so interested in history.

He looked like an old-time preacher with those clothes, I mean red socks and an apricot striped button shirt.

"Frederick Douglass," he recalled, "said this in 1852 on the fourth of July in Rochester, New York: 'What to the American slave is your Fourth of July? I answer: a day that reveals to him, more than all other days in the year, the gross injustice and cruelty to which he is a sham; your boasted liberty, an unholy license; your national greatness, swelling vanity; your sounds of liberty and equality, hollow mockery; your prayers and hymns, your sermons and thanksgivings, with all your religious parade and solemnity, are, to him, more bombast, fraud, deception, impiety and hypocrisy - a thin veil to cover up crimes which would disgrace a nation of savages...'

"Now see," he continued, "Their Fourth of July means nothing to us, we were still in slavery."

"Dad, why are you telling him that?"

"Honey, he needs to know this," granddad said.

"No, he needs to come in the house on time."

"You hear your mother, boy? Huh, I told you, ya'll youngin' are too hardheaded."

"Man..." I said, as grandpa interrupted me.

"Nothing. Take these two books," he said.

He handed me Eldridge Cleaver's "Soul on Ice" and Joseph Conrad's "Lord Jim" and told me to read "Soul on Ice" first.

The vibes in school were as strong as they were on the streets. I fought the knife and came back. I was like a don or something. Jokers looked at me and almost bowed at my presence. I received all kinds of questions. Did it hurt? How was the hospital? Did you think you were going to die, and what did your mom say?

All morning I was like the sun on a cloudy day. "Let me see?" "Can I touch it?" All the attention made me feel weird, like I wasn't human anymore. Out of all the hype, I talked with Ronald about our success with Julius and told him, I got him. We all met in the cafeteria for lunch.

"My mom is lunchin' right now," I told Ant.

"You just got out the hospital, nigga," Ant said.

"Naw, she talking about coming in on time and stuff like that. Hey, and I talked to shorty last night, I mean, I mean."

"Who?" Ronald asked.

"Shorty at the party."

"The same chick that got you stabbed?" Ronald asked.

"She didn't get me stabbed," I said.

"It was her boyfriend, right?" Ronald asked.

"No, she don't mess with him."

"Don't believe that shit," Ant said. "They always say that."

We sat there and talked the whole lunch period. Ronald said he thought he could move water, but he didn't know about the sacks. Ant started shooting spit balls at people. The hip and in crowd didn't eat lunch in the lunch room. This was the first time we sat in here during lunch. I wasn't moving around like I used to, so we made it our chilled spot.

"Stop playing, Ant. You play too much!" A young lady said, wiping her ear.

"That's nasty. Go talk to her or something."

"For what, so she could lie to me?" Ant said.

"Yo, my grandfather hit me with something this morning. For real. He said, the Fourth of July is not really our holiday."

"It's everybody's holiday," Ronald said.

"The way he put it, a lot of Black people were slaves when they celebrated the fourth."

"Man, we helped fight the war that's how we got freed," Ronald said.

"Wrong war," I said.

"Man, Black people did fight in the war and that's the fourth of July. Yo ya'll coming to my game today?"

"Yo, I lost twenty on your last game, why? You want me to tell you, because you can't make lay ups," Ant said.

"You right, but Black people weren't freed because of that war," I said to Ronald.

"Oh, you crazy. Hey Ronald, don't listen to that. First it's Benjamin Franklin. Now, it's the Fourth of July. I tell you what, that's crazy. I tell you something real, nothing matters but money, money, money. Now that's real," Ant said.

"Why it don't matter?"

"Those are the best cook-outs and parties. I don't care if it's on the fourth or the second, I'm there," Ronald said, shaking his shoulders, dancing.

"Who cares? It's time to get money," Ant said.

"Man, I don't care, but I never thought about it. I mean, maybe he just want me to know."

I really never thought about it. The Fourth of July was second to Christmas on my list of holidays. The cook-outs were second to none. The fireworks were by sound a reminder of the sounds of war and by sight a beautiful display of stars and fire. Our family got together and that was good enough. We needed more reasons to get together instead of death or drama. We played basketball, volleyball, kickball, football, cards, you name it and we were doing it on the fourth.

My grandfather was a very old man and I am not sure what his motives were. But what I did know, he had me thinking about stuff people didn't care about.

I was excited about going to class after lunch. I was looking forward to getting back to the hood. *If tonight goes anything like last night, I could pay Julius and we could start stacking some dough*, I thought.

"Welcome back Mr. Larnell," Mr. Binshem said, as I walked in the class. "Would you like to be a fireman, Mr. Larnell."

I shook my head no.

"If you do, you need to thank Benjamin Franklin," he said.

He told the class Benjamin Franklin created the first fire company in America and he thought that he was the true genius of the founding fathers.

He said that Benjamin Franklin was the world's first celebrity.

"I am very concerned about you," Mr. Binshem said to me after class.

"Why is that, Mr. B?" I asked.

"A lot of people here were worried about you. I was shocked when I heard you were in the hospital. You have a lot of ability and I hate to see you waste it."

"I'm all right, Mr. B," I said.

"I don't think so," he said, shaking his head. "There is something going on with you."

"I'm doin' good in your class."

"What about the other classes, Larnell?"

"What you mean?"

"You are failing every class but my class."

"I'm passing English."

"You got a D in English and that's failing, son. Why is that when you have enough ability to do so much more?"

"Mr. B, I know, but those classes..."

"But, but, but, what? You have the ability. There is no excuse. I was very shocked that your grades were so low, very shocked, Larnell."

Mr. Binshem was my favorite. His way of teaching encouraged us to participate and he didn't treat us like the "menace" like Mr. Hawkins did. He made our information relevant and he even tried to perform history.

"You need to think about it. How could you be so close to perfect in this class and fail in all the others? I don't understand."

I sat there for a minute and thought how nice it was to hear someone say you are good in something. I mean, I put my application in at CVS and at least got a below average grade in all my classes. *What is the big deal? I am going to pass*, I thought.

"Are you in a rush?" he asked, packing his bags.

"Naw. What you need, Mr. B?"

"I would like to talk with you more and I need your help with something."

I wanted to say no, but it was Mr. Binshem. I was trying to get to the block and get that money, but I really digged Mr. B. He needed help with something at his home. He said it would take a few hours. I was cool with that. I told Ant and Ronald to meet me on the block later. You know Ant had the ugly look. He was trying to get to the block and so was I.

Mr. Binshem had a gold Honda Accord. His car was clean as a whistle and smelled of vanilla. He threw the black Samsonite brief case in the back and we drove straight to Potomac, Maryland.

We talked about Benjamin Franklin, my neighborhood and history. "Benjamin Franklin is information. He is commerce. He is intellectual; and he is one of the founding fathers of America. He is one of the great ones."

I liked Benjamin Franklin too, but I thought Mr. B was on another level.

I liked when Mr. Binshem used to read from "Poor Richard's Almanac". Just think, he taught humans how to understand electricity. That's a truth that could blow your mind. Electrical power is just as important as concrete.

"Do you know anything about Frederick Douglass?" I asked.

And without hesitation he said, "Frederick Douglass was like the president of Black people in America during his time."

"You know he used to live in Southeast?

"Yes, Mmm."

"My grandfather told me that Frederick Douglass said that the Fourth of July is not for us?"

"Not for whom?" Mr. Binshem asked.

"My grandfather said that Black people were still slaves when America celebrated its independence."

"Well, that's true. But there were a few freed black people up north and Frederick Douglass was one of them."

I don't really know how I felt. I thought independence was the same as Lincoln freeing the slaves.

It kind of meant the same thing to me, when you add the sum of it up; people were celebrating freedom.

My mind was trying to work it out. What did it really mean?

"Frederick Douglass escaped from Baltimore to Philadelphia and he acted like a sailor to get free. Did you know that?" Mr. B, asked.

"A sailor?"

"He had good 'knowledge of ships,' so he talked ship talk. Frederick Douglass was a very smart man. It was written that he was "the noblest slave that ever God set free.""

"Was slave owners Christians too?" I asked. He turned and looked at me and hesitantly said yes.

"Wow, you never hear about that kind of stuff," I said.

"What do you mean?"

"Like stuff about the Fourth and slave owners were followers of Jesus," I said.

"History is good for learning about the past, but not for creating negative feelings," he said.

"I am just confused right now. I've been to Sunday school and the stuff you hear bout slavery don't go with what I hear bout Jesus."

"That's a good point," he said.

I could hear Ant saying, "Stay out the dream world. It don't really matter."

I mean, Benjamin Franklin and Frederick Douglass are dead and the slaves are as well.

We drive cars and have microwaves. I mean, money is the common denominator for all cultures. So, as long as I kept making ends, I wouldn't have to deal with history and its uneven truths. Mr. Binshem and my grandfather had me thinking. I wouldn't even be able to play PlayStation, if it wasn't for electricity.

We pulled up in front of a house, a grand single-family mansion, grass cut like a fresh shape up. The walkway was marble and slate to the door.

Flowers and evergreens decorated the landscape. A Mercedes 500 series had residence in the driveway. When I walked in, it was like, "which way do I go, which way do I go?" The man had statues in the living room and a dining room table that sat twelve people.

A woman came from out the back with papers in her hand. Her black hair was cut even and touched her shoulders. She had on a skirt suit with two inch heels and a Versace scarf around her neck. She was very beautiful and stood stately.

"Honey," Mr. B, said, "this is Larnell, the student I was telling you about."

"Hi," she said, "he talks about you so much. It's good to meet you."

I shook her hand and said, "Hi." She was like a movie star or something. She walked in with mad grace and strength, looking at First Class mail.

"Larnell, this is my wife Cathy," Mr. Binshem said. She asked him to pick their daughter up from Regatta practice and that she was going to the mall to get Anna a gift.

"Like whoa. Mr. Binshem's living big and he's only a teacher," I thought.

"Sometimes, I wonder about you," Mr. B, said.

Before I could say a word, Mr. B, said, "Not only me, there are many people in the school that like you. You are a real intelligent guy."

You get excellent grades in my class and fail the others. It doesn't make a lot of sense. The question you asked me about Christians, you don't hear those kinds of questions from children your age."

We sat there and talked about the hood. He asked questions about my family and talked about his family. He told me that he was a lawyer and that his wife was a lawyer as well. He thought it was a tragedy that most Black youth live without a mother and a father in the home.

"Well, that's normal in my community," I said. I didn't have one friend with a father in the house.

He said he practiced law for twenty-five years and was a partner when he left.

He thought he would use his talent to help those who needed it the most. I hope the talent he was talking about wasn't his acting.

"My grandfather is like a father to me," I said.

"That's good. Grandparents try to keep the family in order," he said.

"Gettin' on your nerves," I said.

"Your grandfather is probably the one who helped your mind. You have a very good mind," he said.

I just looked straight ahead. "I have a good mind." I have a good mind to make that money. Mr. B, is living like Don King and driving a Honda. The carpet in his house felt like a four inch mattress.

He knew more about my people than I did. He told me never to give up. Deep down inside I thought, give up on what? On the way back to the hood, he gave me his numbers and told me not to hesitate to call if I needed someone to talk to.

He didn't ask for help with anything, so maybe he wanted to just know about my family and how I was living. Anxiety was all over his face. I told him that I was ok. I know I just got stitches in my back, but I had to defend myself.

"You got a fireplace in your dining room? That's all right." I said, trying to change the mood.

"You're called to the principal's office too much," Mr. B,

said. "You could do better." Speech is ok, but then what? I can't even get in CVS, but Julius let me in and in one night, I made more than a thousand dollars. Now how do you suppose I get the figures?

As we approached my hood, I asked him to take me to the parking lot. There were a few people loitering. I didn't see Ant or Ronald, as I got out the car. I couldn't get two steps away from Mr. B's car, before a head from the night asked, "You got that? That shit was good!"

"What!?" I said, with my eyes guiding caution to the car, A'ight, Mr. B. I'll see you tomorrow. Thanks."

In the circle I noticed Steve hugging a tree.

"Come on, Steve," someone said.

Steve was hugging the tree very tight, tears flowing down his face.

"Don't touch him," Julius said.

"What I do, Julius? What I do?" Steve asked, crying.

"You didn't do nothing," Julius said.

"I," Steve screamed. "Stop.. okay... okay, I."

"Steve, what the fuck?" Larry asked.

"The snakes," he said crying.

"What snakes?" Julius asked.

"He high as a motherfucker," Rock said.

"Do something," someone said in the crowd.

"Do what? Laugh at his ass? That's what I'm going to do," Rock said.

"No, no, to you," Steve said.

"To who, Steve? Get off the damn tree. Where is Wembo?" Julius said. "I want him off that tree. Rock, two-way Wembo and tell him to come here."

He was talking about snakes and I didn't see a worm. White saliva was all over his mustache and beard. He was crying like a child against the mom's belt. Rock was laughing, calling him the resident pipe head.

"You can have it," Steve yelled, fearfully.

"Yo Steve, cool out. What's up?" I said.

"My clothes..!" he said.

Larry tried to get Steve off the tree but he was too strong. The hold on the tree was like concrete to a bridge.

"Get him some milk," someone said.

"Hey Steve, what up man?" I asked

"L," he said, shaking his head, "I.. They want me. They want me!"

"They want you? Who want you?"

Julius asked Wembo to get Steve off the tree. Wembo went to grab Steve and was fought off. Steve was about five eight and Wembo about six three. Wembo managed to pull Steve from the birch tree and Steve got low and came up and knocked Wembo two feet back. Wembo looked at him, took a deep breath and with his big hands grabbed Steve again. Steve hollered, "No!"

"What the...?" Ant said as he and Ronald walked up.

"Why they fighting?" Ronald asked.

"Steve lunchin'," I said.

Steve broke loose from Wembo and ripped off his t-shirt.

"Here," he said crying, take it, I..."

As Wembo was going at him again, Julius told him to hold fast.

"This nigga is lunchin'," Rock said.

"Fuckin' pipe head," Larry said.

"No," Steve said, unbuckling his pants.

The block once again began to fill. The neighbors and heads alike came to the show.

"Steve, I got to get you in," Julius said.

"Damn," Ronald said.

Again whispers, chatter and the sounds of humans in awe took hold.

Steve stood there and took off his belt.

"I am sorry, Julius. I am sorry!" Steve pleaded.

He took his toe, flipped his heel, and his left shoe came off. The next thing I knew, Steve was trying to take off his pants.

"Get him Wembo," Julius commanded.

Wembo charged at Steve. Steve broke down the street with his pants under his butt. I was in amazement. "What the hell is Steve doing?" His pants were continuing to fall. He had no shirt on and his pants were falling by the second. Wembo took long steps, but Steve and his mini steps seemed faster.

"Oh, shit," Ronald said laughing.

I could not believe Steve was acting like that. Maybe it was the sun and the heat that made him spin out of control. I just knew he was my man. He helped me get that flow. Now he was running down the street with his pants down to his knees.

"Call the ambulance," someone said.

I wanted to run behind him. He was out of his mind and maybe a friendly face or voice could bring him back.

Wembo got hold of him and put him in a Hulk Hogan brace lock.

One of the neighborhood girls gave him some milk as Wembo held on. Steve was kicking like an engine running off vapors.

As Wembo was taking him to the apartment, my sister walked up and said, "Robin called and grandpa is looking for you. Can I have five dollars?"

"Damn, was he off the boat?" Ronald asked.

"He was off more than the boat," Ant said.

I didn't know what it was, but I thought, it was the wrong time for him to trip out. He was our man and helped us get settled.

"Money is coming. So what did your teacher want?" Ant asked.

"We talked. He didn't ask me to do anything. I know one

thing; he is living like he's rich."

"Where you go?"

"We went to his house, out Potomac somewhere. Hey, Rock could I see you phone for a minute?" I said.

"Potomac? Damn. How that joint look?" Ronald asked.

"Sshh, the carpet in the joint is like three inches thick," I said, dialing Robin. "Mr. B is living like he on TV or something."

"Hey," I said, as Robin picked up her phone.

"Hey, were you at school today?"

"Yeah."

"You didn't say anything to me. Where were you at lunchtime?"

"The lunchroom."

"You not taking the SAT prep class?"

"What?"

"You said you were going to take the prep class with me."

"Robin, what are you talking about? I didn't say that."

"Are you coming over here today?"

"Naw, I got something to do."

"You got something to do?" she asked, sarcastically.

"Look, man I'll call you back."

"Larnell," she called.

"Yes?"

"What time?"

"Robin, I got to handle something. I will get back at you in a minute," I said, as I hung the phone up.

I gave Ronald fifty sacks and a bottle of the green. We found out Steve took one of our sacks and smoked it. He probably had an Old English 800 too. All three of us sat on the block and talked for a while and pushed our product. It wasn't like when Steve was with us, but we got our message across.

We called it "Mazon Crazon" our brand, our label, and it was inspired by Steve. Ronald changed his mind and felt that he could sell sacks instead of the bottles.

I told him that Julius said it was better to start that way. Julius said, "You have a better understanding of the street when you're on the street."

Even a bad night was good on the block. This was a huge jump from fives and tens. We didn't need to go to the store for Mrs. Parker for them Jimmy Deans. We were letting them know, "If you want a trip like Steve, come get this boat, the Mazon Crazon."

Rock was very uptight about Mag and his crew. He told one dude he had to wait to make a sale and ain't nobody say a word. Mag and his crew were around, but they lived in the circle.

"We do the same thing. I don't like these bums. They came off wrong from the beginnin'," Rock said.

Rock told us to watch them and to keep our eyes open. He also told us, that they kept Don Don and that he may be gone for good.

Mag or Don Don didn't really matter to us. We were trying to stack some cash and big cuz made that possible. Ronald went home and Ant and me stayed out there pushing and pounding the block. "It's here, it's here. The Mazon Crazon. Take your trip. We got it right here.

Over the next few weeks Ant and myself, with Julius's help, managed to stack over twelve thousand dollars. I don't know how much Ronald had, but he was moving more than anybody.

We had networked our business as Julius suggested. We had Abdul in Valley Green, Moe in Barry Farms, Kwon Uptown, Topsoldier in Eastgate and William up Penn St, NE. Our clientele got large day by day. We had half the city talking about the "Sons of Caesar" and that "Mazon Crazon."

Chapter

9

Gettin' it and
the Ungrateful

The showers of April covered the neighborhood.
Nature's elements have a way of slowing down all
movement. I sat there on porch with both pant legs rolled up
over my Adidas, I was thinking about tomorrow. It was time
for go-go and rap to come together again and RADIO
ONE's 93 WKYS was hosting the party. Julius had the
tickets and we had been counting the days down like the
twelve days before Christmas and time had come.

While the rain was reinforcing dew and its purpose the
neighborhood retreated to shelter and sleep. The grind was
too sweet for Ant and I. We liked the rain. The people who
weren't sleeping were getting high.

As Ant and I stood under the porch overhead Ronald was
trying to put a plastic trash bag over his scooter. Ant and I
didn't have a scooter. We had two twenty-four speed
Schwinn bikes and book bags. We made all deliveries and
drops with those twin wheels.

Rock was out there with his seamen's rain coat and
Wembo was just standing, with no hat on. He looked like a
big Black ape — like a Silverback in the Congo Mountain in

a tropical rain shower, just mute.

Mag was out there sitting in a black Maxima with a couple of dudes.

"Hi, L," a woman said, smiling. "You getting big. This is my cousin ReRe."

"What up?" I said, rubbing my stomach.

"You don't see nobody else?" Ant said.

"I wasn't talking to you," she said.

"I was talkin' to you."

She smacked her lips and asked, "L, do you got anything? Rock said you did." I sold her five for sixty dollars, because I liked her and she was one of Julius's friends.

The grind was slow and steady in the rain. Cee Cee was about five years older than us. She was light skinned and bow legged. She walked very sexy.

"It's that 'Mazon Crazon'," I said.

"Is it? I'll see you later," she said, flirtatiously.

My pockets had more than seven hundred dollars in them, before my man Kwon came by for ten one ounce joints and we made a quick three grand off that. The block was like a moving flea market. The more money you had the better the deal.

"Yeah?" I said, answering my cell phone.

"What are you doing?" Robin asked.

"Hoping this rain stop, so I could go up Georgetown."

"Are you coming over here later?"

"Yeah, later."

"Is Ant and Ronald there?"

"Yea, Ant over there shaking dice, and Ronald is doing something with his chain. Yo, Robin said hey."

"Ask her is she coming to the party?" Ronald asked, laughing.

Jokingly she said, "Sure, what time should I be there?"

Robin didn't go out. She was the neighborhood choir girl. She stayed in church. She's been my girlfriend for more than a year and the prettiest Hershey kiss in the neighborhood.

When the rain slowed, we walked up Mississippi Avenue, Southeast, then hit Nineteenth Street to Savannah. Ronald had two blunts and we gulped them down like water flowing down a mountain.

"I don't have nothin'," Ant said, talking to someone on his cell phone.

"Who that? What they need? I got something!" Ronald sung.

"Why you so excited," said Ant. "We on Savannah. Two bottles?"

"I ain't got no bottles," Ronald said.

"Tell him to catch Kwon. I just gave him a few bottles," I said.

I was about high as a kite when we got on the 32 bus.

"We got to get a car, man," Ant said.

"I feel ya," I said. "But Julius said wait until we have thirty sitting. Let's do this last sixth and see what he says."

"We walkin' and ridin' bikes with G's in our pockets. In a minute, somebody is goin' to try us. And I swear I'm goin' to straight jack anybody who get out of line!" Ant said.

"Calm down."

"You know what Ant? You got a problem," Ronald said. "Here, take this magic marker and write your problems on the bus seat or we could smoke on it."

"Why I got a problem?"

"Cause, man, you be buggin'," Ronald said.

My mind drifted back to history again. Thinking now, we rushed to the back of the bus. A long time ago that was the only place blacks were allowed to sit.

I got the marker from Ronald and put my name on the seat. I wrote, "L from SE was here, but now I am gone. I left my name to carry on, if you know very well, I got that Mazon Crazon wit the good smell."

Ant did have a problem, but I understood it somewhat. His only brother died from AIDS. As the story goes, he was a married man and his wife had an affair with another man. This man had promiscuous relationships with men and women. And as it went, caught the HIV virus and gave it to Ant's brother's wife. So, Ant had an edge.

"Y'all need to get a moped," Ronald said. "I gets around, son."

"No exercise. You ride around looking like a mailman. But what's wrong with me? You can't even make a lay-up and you think somethin' is wrong wit me," Ant asked.

"You be lunchin'. You just be lunchin'. Look, when we get off this bus, we gonna smoke this joint to the head and get to the bottom of it."

"Forget you, you non lay-up makin'. You the only six-four nigga in hood can't play basketball," Ant said.

I was looking out the window as the bus turned onto Pennsylvania Avenue, Southeast. I got lost in the views and sights from the windows. Anacostia Park lay under the bridge as we approached Potomac Gardens.

The bus moved northwest but was still in Southeast. I saw black faces all over, young baby mothers pushing strollers. People milling about, going in and out the Chinese joints and the local clothing stores, but as the bus approached Capitol Hill, the complexion of the people began to change.

I took note as I was high as a kite that this bus came straight from my hood and now, we were passing the nation's capitol with the 'twin-shelled iron dome,' the same one that was completed by President Lincoln. We passed the Library of Congress and came within blocks of the Supreme Court. As the bus passed west of the Capitol, the complexions changed to completely white.

There were families walking with cameras, bags, and children on their father's backs. The whole family, it seemed, wore sunglasses traveling to our museums and national monuments.

"Look at all these people," I said.

"Forget those people. I am trying to find out why he act the way he do," Ronald said.

"I'll tell you why, ain't nothing funny, it's time to get that money. Oh, ya'll like the way I said that?" Ant said.

"Yeah, yeah that was nice," Ronald said. "I could make a flow for you, son. Check it. Check it. I'm Ronald, the dancing man. Like to take the pretty ladies by the hand. They say oh, he so cool, I say yeah, I'll take you from your dude.

Check it, check it. I'm on the metro bus headed up G town 'bout to get that fly gear so I could put it down!"

"Yeah, ok, I'm Ant and the ladies look at me and I will kick them in their face, yeah."

"See, that's what I mean," Ronald said.

"It's time we hook you up because kicking the pretties in the face, that's not goin' to do."

"Forget him L make a flow,"

"I am L/I wear Top Tens. Sportin' 'em all over/'bout to get these ends. I make no fuss and I don't holla ya see/love the ladies, history, oh did I forget me/Me flow? DC. Act like you know, down here we party to the Go-Go. Yo, check, I flipped a flow but I can't party unless they go-go."

"Oh, I like that, but you still can't do like me, young rookie."

"I took SE/ the lyrics to another range, I sell these bottles and sacks, stump down and stack my change, out of range. I, It's me that MC, microphone check. Mazon Crazon got the MC twisted, blisted. Ya can't mess with this, see. I'll give you the dance like Usher, the flow like Jay-Z, yeah it's the R-O-N-A-L-D there is no flow in DC that could fuck with me."

A few people on the bus took note of the hip-hop

session. By this time the complexion of the bus even changed. The bus was making its way past the White House.

Black and white alike smiled as they caught view of the metro bus hip-hop cipher.

"Do you write that down," one lady asked.

"I don't have to, but I do sometimes," Ronald said, shaking his head as if he had ear phones on.

By the time we got to Georgetown, the bus was completely white. I saw it happen right before my eyes. I mean the bus started out with all black people and ended up with all white people. This must be what they talk about when they say desegregated segregation. I mean, I saw it happen right before my eyes.

We spent as we always do. Ant and Ronald did more of their shopping at the Hugo Boss shop this time, but I made deals with Faprilo. I even got a pair of Timberlands (Butters) and a pair of Super Star Adidas.

"I see cloudy skies don't stop the ladies from comin' out," Ronald said.

"It sure don't," I said, as my cell phone rang. "What up?"

"You," Kim said.

"We up G-town."

"Buy me something."

"What ya want?" I asked.

"A pair of Gucci shoes."

"Ok, are you goin' to the party this weekend?" I asked.

"Yeah, I need like three tickets."

"I'll give you one, but your friends are goin' pay."

We walked M Street to hail a cab. A car drove up beside us pumping Julius's commercial on 93.9 WKYS.

"I can't wait!" Ronald said.

"Man, he got that joint on the radio," Ant followed.

"Y'all know we goin' pass out flyers this weekend," I said.

"I don't care as long as I get into the party, cause everybody in the city gonna be there. You think your cuz could set me up with P-Diddy," Ronald asked.

"For what?" Ant asked while trying to hail the cab.

"You heard my flows, son."

"Man, if one more cab pass me, I'm goin' to bust they fuckin' window!" Ant said.

"Man, chill out," I said.

"Naw. What? We got all these bags. Look they picking everybody else up."

"I'm not getting' on the bus wit' all these bags," Ronald said.

"We don't have to get on the bus. Look," I said, as I stood and took off my hat.

I walked in the street with bags in hand. I waved for the next cab coming our way on M Street.

The cab was empty and it didn't have an "out of service" sign in the window. He passed us by like we were a pile of defecation. No one laughed when he stopped a block away to pick up someone else. I felt like a hunting dog, who wasn't worthy of the master's house. Talk about self-esteem; I couldn't because at that very moment I had none.

I couldn't compare it to anything, not even being followed in a department store. The emptiness I felt and the bold disrespect caused anger to build inside. A quick glance of hatred penetrated deep. I found myself fighting with the concept of right and wrong.

"I hate them motherfuckers!" I said.

"Man, I swear," Ant said, as he went in the trash can and pulled out a McDonald's bag, candy paper and two bottles. One was a 22oz Heineken and the other, a bottle of Beringer's White Zinfandel.

"Ronald, try to get one. If they don't stop, I'm a fuck 'em up," Ant continued.

"Stop lunchin'," I said. "Forget 'em. I'll call someone to get us."

Ronald tried to call another but it rolled on by.

"Man, what! See, see," he said, running toward the cab with bottle in hand.

"Shit!" Ronald said as Ant threw the Beringer's bottle. The bottle shattered the cab's back window. The car came to an immediate stop. Backed up and the driver got out, but Ant was running toward the car with the Heineken - in hand.

"I'll break your fuckin' head, bitch!" Ant yelled.

My eyes almost popped out my head.

The cabby jumped back in his cab and pulled off.

"What! What!" Ant said.

Laughing, Ronald said, "O, my God, is this shit real?"

"So what? What, they think my money ain't green? Look! My money green," he said, pulling out a sack of Benjamin's.

What seemed like seconds later, we heard the sirens coming from everywhere. We took off and ran up Twenty-Eighth Street. I was nervous, I called Julius. And I'm glad I did. He told me to get to Twenty-Eighth and Dumbarton and go in Wally's Market. "Tell Mr. Wally you're Buck's grandson and he'll safe house you," Julius said.

"Man, for real, what's wrong with you?" Ronald asked. "But naw, you see how he jumped back in the cab, man. That was some funny shit."

"So what?" Ant said.

"You need to stop actin' crazy. I'm not tryin' to get locked up over no stupid cabs and shit!" I said.

"Man, we need a car," Ant said, "cause I'm not trippin'."

While running through the streets I took notice of the small historic homes that comprise Georgetown. They were very small from the outside. A lot of them still had areas for horses and buggies.

As I entered the store, I did what Julius told me to do. The white man at the counter didn't say a word. He just nodded and directed us to a room in the back.

"What if the police would have caught us?" I asked.

"Yeah, man. I'm trying to go to the party and you throwing bottles at people," Ronald said.

"Naw, for real, they gonna take our money, lock us up. Find out our spot, makin' everything hot. Because what? A cab didn't want to take us home."

"That's not the point," Ant said.

"No, the point is we got to use our heads. Fuck them cabs, for real," I said.

All of our intentions were honest. We just wanted to get a ride home. You get the sickest feeling when a taxi just passes you by. It makes you feel like you are nothing.

I felt like Ant, really. But I couldn't get myself to throw a bottle. Who do those African cab drivers think they are? I thought. Yeah, my ancestors were servants and slaves in the colonies.

But does that give them the right to pass me by. The very ones who could tell us something of our past ride right pass us with their noses up. Africa is carved up like a vegetable garden while they fight over invisible lines, but they look at me screw face. The black continent has been raped and turned out to be a whore. But they look at me screw face.

The worst feelings started going through my mind. Like how I hate cab drivers. The worst part was that they were people of color. And as soon as they see a white man, they cause accidents, make illegal turns and sudden stops. It made me so mad. How can they just overlook me? Who gave them the right? They could stop and say, "I can't go to Southeast."

"I ain't trippin'," Ant said.

"I'm trippin'," Ronald said, "Nigga, we got tickets to the biggest party in the city and you want to throw bottles at cars?"

Chapter

10

Attacking
Pawns

Julius sent Rock to pick us up. While they were getting ready to watch game five of the Bulls and Pacers, I took Ronald's moped and went over Kim's house.

Kim lived in a nice little house on Varney. When I pulled up, she was in her gate talking to someone in a car. The car pulled off when I got off the bike.

"Who's that?" I asked, handing her the stuff.

"No one," she said.

"No one? Was it that nigga?" I asked.

"No. Come here. You crack me up," she said, pulling me closer and kissing my neck.

"Like what, your grandmother in there?"

"No. You got the tickets?"

"Naw, I ain't got no tickets," I said.

"Calm down," she said, sitting on the porch.

Her legs were glowing brighter than the sun and they were smooth as a baby's butt. She had on a blue skirt and a red tank top. Her toes were painted red and looked so pretty, real pretty. She had the kind of feet you kiss. Sitting in her flip flops they looked better than paint on skittles and I imagined that they would taste even better. She was just plain beautiful. You could spend a half day just looking at her.

While I was standing on the porch looking at her legs, she opened them.

"You got underwear on?" I asked.

"Come see," she said.

"It would be my pleasure," I mumbled under my breath.

"What you say?"

I introduced my index finger to her moist inner lips and kissed her all over.

"Come on," she said, holding my hand. We walked in the house and I said, "Hold on. This is special. Could we just sit on the couch for a minute?"

"No, boy."

"Just a kiss," I said, like a strong puppy making sure the rubber was in my pocket.

On grand-mom's couch, we kissed and I held on to her like the government does Fort Knox. Grand-mom's couch was orange and purple with carnation flowers in the pattern. There was a red and orange throw rug on the floor. It all worked with the end tables, with the yellow, red and orange vases and fake flowers. Jesus' picture was on the wall. The same Lord that some say Michael Angelo painted to please the western world.

Upstairs we played grown up. Dancing in the nude, the moist lips held me. When people say "fit like a glove," that couldn't describe the feeling. I felt like I met Pocahontas. I thought about rocks, the moped, her old dresser and anything that would keep my mind off the feeling and her. It was all about work. That's right, I wanted to put work in and work I did.

It wasn't her noise; I didn't hear it. I was on the rocks, but when she said, "My leg never shook like that," I thought I did something special. She continued to rub my arms and kiss my chest.

"Are you going to give me the tickets?" she asked softly.

"I don't have them right now."

"You lying. Y'all don't have tickets to that joint?"

It was time for me to go. I got up and put on my clothes.

"Where you going," she asked.

"I got business."

"Are you going to give me the tickets?"

"What I say? I don't have the tickets right now, but your girls gonna pay."

She looked at me and rolled her eyes.

"What? I'm supposed to pay your girls' way, too? I'm payin your way."

"I don't wanna talk about it."

"What?" I said.

"We'll get in there. I don't need you."

"What! I'm gone, I'll talk with you later," I said, walking out.

I didn't get it. I did something real serious, but she had tripped out on me. How do I owe her friends? Forget it, I thought, as I took the moped over Robin's house.

Robin lived on First and South Capitol Street, Southeast. Her apartment building stood on a corner. Robin and I had the classic relationship— the good girl, bad guy. She wasn't into going out to parties or kissing. She didn't care about the latest fashion and she was one of the smartest people I knew, after my grandfather and Mr. Binshem.

"Hi, Ms. Wilkinson," I said, to Robin's mother as she answered the door.

"How are you, Larnell?" She asked.

"Cool," I said.

"Hey," Robin said, as she entered the living room and gave me a hug. The Cosby Show was on TV.

"Are you going to church with me and my mother this weekend?" Robin asked.

"For what? When?" I felt like I was going to have an anxiety attack. She stressed me out about church. She pressed me about it over an over.

"Because you missed Easter," she said.

"The party is this Saturday," I said.

"Church is in the morning. My mother asked me to ask you."

"I don't know if I could make it."

"Why not?"

"Where the cards at, man?" I asked, to get past the issue.

"I don't want to play cards. Eh mom," she called. She told her mother what I said.

She went right for my weakness, her mother. Her mother was lively and very nice, but told me right out, if I wanted to see her daughter, then she needed to be in the house by dark.

"Could you put the game on?" I asked.

I never heard of people going to church on Saturdays, not until I met Robin.

The National News reported, "King's Widow Offers Reno 'New Evidence' Of Conspiracy."

"Ray didn't act alone," a prominent African American said, while being interviewed.

"You see that?" I said.

"What?" Robin asked. She didn't hear one thing the reporter said. The TV was on, but she didn't hear it. She was too worried about me going to church on a Saturday.

"Larnell," her mother called. "sweetie, what are you doing Saturday morning?"

"Umm, nothin'," I answered.

"Good, I'll pick you up at 9:00 a.m." she said.

That's all Robin needed to hear as her face lit up, "I'll play cards now," she said.

"All right. Can you turn the game on? You real slick, but that's cool. How long is church? I mean, like, I got something to do Saturday. I hope it's not all day."

"I'm glad you're going. You're starting to change," she said.

"Let's play five hundred, and stop acting like my mother," I said.

She turned on the NBA playoffs and Chicago was beating the mess out of the Pacers. The Pacers won two straight games and all bets were that Michael Jordan and the Bulls were done. However, in game five, Michael's twenty-nine points had the Bulls up by 31 at the end of the third period.

It was a done deal.

I wasn't the biggest basketball fan, but I liked to play it. Basketball was the only sport you could play anywhere. We played it on the playground, swinging over poles in the woods with a milk crate nailed to a tree; in the street with a 12-inch bike rim nailed to a utility pole. We even used each other as the board and rim, and a lot of faces were bruised. We would make a basketball court in the house by opening an iron hanger and positioning it between the door and frame.

"Where the cards at?" I asked Robin.

"Why you got a cell phone and beeper?" she asked.

"I be kind of busy now," I said.

She shook her head, "That's why you need to go to church."

"Church for what!"

"Pastor Wilbon teaches and my church is nice."

"Let me teach you something. Answer this question. When is Independence Day for Black people?"

"Fourth of July," she answered.

"Wrong."

"No, I will tell you when, it's the day they meet Jesus," she answered.

"Michael Jordan!" the announcer yelled. "He's got to be

the greatest player of all time."

When you look at Michael Jordan "The Middle Passage" is but a fable. How could he be a descendent from the world's greatest human cargo? He is a God and doing things unthinkable. He's a great man walking the earth, like a son of the great Aten or the great Zeus but never from the ancestors of Africa.

Looking at him perform with such grace and balance was like watching the "greatest show on earth."

My phone started ringing and Robin gave me the look.

"Hello," I said.

"You need to get back!" Ant said.

"What up?"

"One of Mag dudes beat the shit out of Steve and Rock is on a nut."

"Where is Julius?" I asked.

"He out here somewhere. Hey, Ronald said bring his bike too. Hurry up."

"I'll be there in a minute," I said.

"See, that's why you need church. You got to go be somewhere," she said.

"I'm goin' to church!" I said, annoyed.

She rolled her eyes, "I guess you got to go now," she said, with a joyless face. I felt the melancholy. It was in the air and I couldn't do anything about it. My man Ant called. The block had drama, and I had to go.

Looking at Robin's face, I saw concern and love. She didn't even walk me to the door.

I approached the block. The human arena wasn't hard to find with the noise. I drove the bike over the curb, onto the side walk. Pushing the gas and the brake, I cautiously scanned the crowd. Then I hit the gas, the wheels spinning.

"Man, give me my bike," Ronald said, as dust flew. When I looked around I heard Rock say, "I don't wanna hear that shit!" Larry was pushing him through the crowd with Ant following.

"Yo," Ant said to me. "Dude beat the shit out of Steve."

"Hear, what?" The dude said, "like I said, he owes me money."

"Why the fuck he still talkin'?" Rock asked.

I looked around for my cousin and I saw Mag talking to another alien. Every day there was a new face on the block and they all seemed to be coming from Mag's coattail.

As the commotion picked up, I noticed Mag and Tony pointing and smiling. They were looking our way.

"Who the fuck they smilin' at? I'm sick of that nigga," Ant said, looking their way, spitting.

"Where Julius at?"

"He got Steve somewhere," someone said.

"Hey, yo. Leave that shit alone," I said.

I called Julius and told him Rock and one of Mag's boy's was about to get into it. "I know. Stay cool. Rock and Larry will handle it," he said.

Julius was the reason for Ronald's moped, my cell phone and a lot of the wealth we experienced on the block and he told me to "stay cool." Rock's and Ant's attitude toward Mag and his crew was getting out of hand. Since Mag and his family lived around our way, I really didn't see a problem.

What I did know, Julius was the leader and Mag was the alien with his own power and wealth. Slowly but surely Mag was stacking the block with his homies and Rock was very agitated. But, like Julius said, "Stay cool. We are gonna get business that's goin' to help us move to the right of these streets."

He was our walking example and many people looked up to him in our hood. He knew people from all walks of life. One call today and he managed to get us out of the screaming sirens' way. He made all of this possible, even my fat pockets.

"I told ya don't come around here wit' that shit!" Rock said.

"That's between Steve and dude," Larry said.

"Larry, I don't wanna hear that shit ya talkin'."

"Do me like that," Rock said, pointing his finger at the dude, while Larry stood between the two.

"What happened?" I asked.

"Steve owe dude money," Ant said.

"You seen my cousin?" I asked again.

"They was over there. They say Steve got beat down."

"Did anybody help him?" I asked.

"Rock stopped it," Ronald said.

"Owe him money for what?" I asked.

"They bet on the Bulls and Pacers game. Steve didn't have the money. Dude punched Steve in the mouth and knocked his teeth out too. Rock been goin' off on Mag and his whole crew. I thought they were goin' to go to blows for a second," Ronald said.

"I hate them niggas," Ant said and then screamed, "Fuck all you niggas!"

"Oh lord, I'm gone. Y'all niggas crazy. Y'all need some music. Ant, there you go again. It's over a basketball game. The same reason Melvin got killed, remember?" Ronald said.

I heard the punch, a loud crack like he broke a bone in dudes face. I looked around and dude was falling to the ground.

"Hold up!" someone yelled while Rock was trying to jump on top of him.

One of Mag's boys jumped on Rock as Larry held him. Ant jumped on dude and then I heard powdow! Powdow! It sounded like canon fire.

My heart went straight to my shoes, but not faster than

I went to the ground. All the wrestling stopped as the human arena scattered. While low, I looked around to see if anyone was hit and where the shots came from.

"Wrong mon, wrong mon," Mag said.

Larry managed to get Rock off dude after the two blasts. No one was hit. The dude with Mag shot the gun.

"Fuck you. You think we don't have guns? I told ya not to come around with that shit," Rock said.

"You want fight?" Mag asked.

"Naw, naw," Larry said.

"I'll beat your ass. Fuck you!" Rock said, pulling out his gun.

"No guns, never me mon. Nah good to hit mi mon like that. Fair one on one, mon," Mag said, as dude took off his shirt.

"What?" Rock asked.

"Naw, naw," Larry said. "No fighting. Fuck that, Rock."

"Beat his ass, Rock. Beat his ass!" Ant said.

I wasn't ready to fight and I didn't want to see the hospital again. I knew I had to man up and get ready for what ever the drama brought my way.

While Ant walked closer to Rock and Larry, I stood there looking at the dude who shot the gun.

How could he come around here and shoot his gun? This situation was getting out of control day by day. I was beginning to understand what Rock was talking about.

In a time when fist fighting had lost its glory to the rules of the Wild West, Rock and Mag's man was about to go head to head.

"Do me like that. Fuck you!" Rock said.

"Let's go," Dude said.

"Watch this, bitch!" Rock said, as he threw jab blows to dude's head. Dude bull-rushed and grabbed Rock and they fell. He went for Rock's neck, when he got flipped. But Rock let him up, just to tap on his dome.

Mag's face was twisted with disgust. He looked on while his boy got beat down. How could he just watch this? I would never watch anyone beat Ant down like that. Even the dude with the gun sat mute beside Mag and didn't make a move. Even in my condition, I would've at least broken it up.

"I'm gonna beat your ass. Get up, bitch!" Rock said.

Dude got up and screamed, "Fuck you." Then Rock went in close and tagged him with a hook to the body and one hard one to the jaw and dude dropped from Rock's air space.

"Yeah," Ant said.

"Damn, he sharp as shit!" Ronald said.

"Take his ID," Ant said.

One-on-one fights were not even heard of. I don't think I saw one since I was nine years old and at sixteen it seemed foreign. It was crew against crew, gun against gun and knife against knife, times that reminded me of cowboys and the towns they ruled with the gun.

Dude's eye and mouth were bloody.

"Throw in the towel before he kills this dude. Somebody throw in the towel," Ant said.

"That's enough, Rock," Larry said.

"Where's the towel? Beat that nigga's ass, 'til I see a towel," Ant said.

"Ant, cool out," I said.

"That nigga can fight, man," Ronald said.

"I didn't know he could fight like that." I said.

"He took those dudes off you at the party. He was knocking them out. Hey, I need to re-up tomorrow," Ronald said, before he took off.

"Yeah, I know, but I didn't see him throw any punches. See how he hittin' 'em? Man, he look like he box," I said.

"Put your hand on somebody else around here and I'll beat your ass," Rock yelled.

Dude just looked up. I couldn't believe Mag and his boys. They just let him get beat down. The whipping was brutal albeit, one on one, I couldn't watch my man fall without helping him up.

Rock let it be known from day one that he had a problem with immigrants. His attitude toward those dudes got worse by the day. Somebody had to know that he wasn't going for anything.

"Come on Rock," Larry said, grabbing one of his arms.

Up in the apartment, Cee Cee was nursing Steve. He had a mouse on his eye and a missing tooth. Julius was on the phone and Wembo was standing by the door.

"He lucky, L. He lucky," Steve said.

"Who lucky Steve?" I asked.

"I couldn't punch," Steve said.

"You couldn't or you didn't?" I asked.

Steve frowned. "What you mean, L?"

"Could've, should've, would've," Larry interjected. "If you wasn't a stupid junkie, you wouldn't bet money you don't have."

"Dude didn't have no business puttin' his hands on Steve. They know Steve our man; that's no regard. That's no regard for Julius. What they sayin' fuck Julius?" Rock said, walking to the kitchen.

"That's some shit. The game just went off and he punched you already. So what the fuck is that? Fuck them niggas. The game just went off, Rock. For real, Rock. It just went off," Ant said.

"For real, though," Cee Cee said. "He wanted to fight Steve anyway."

"Man, look. Steve is his own man. He made the bet so he should deal with it," Larry said.

"I messed up, L. Right, L? Hey L, I messed up, huh? He just hit me. I was about to do something too," Steve said.

"They think they could come around here and do what

they want. I'm going to end up fuckin' that nigga Mag up,"
Rock said.

"Man, you out of control," Larry said.

"Larry, you could've gave him the money, but you just let
dude punch him in the face. That's bullshit," Rock said.

"No, you could've gave him the money. You was out
there," Larry said.

Steve was the neighborhood's non-violent flunky and to
be correct, he was Julius's flunky. He did just about anything
you asked.

He smoked drugs, but he had a good heart. I felt sorry
for him with his face twisted and bruised. He was the only
one out the crew that was satisfied with life and getting high.

He didn't have a lot of issues, like me and Ant. We
wanted money and anyway we could get it. Larry was the
softest out the group. That's at least what me and Ant
thought. Rock wanted to fight everybody. Wembo had a
family, paid rent, and was the quietest out of them all. But
his eyes, Julius said, were like that of eagles.

Steve, on the other hand, didn't pay rent nowhere. He
stayed with Julius or was put up by Julius. He didn't have any
children and he knew every street head in Southeast. He did
ten years in Lorton and didn't beef with anyone. You could
smack him around, call him names and he would take it.

Julius was very fond of him; everyone knew that. It was
like Steve was his adopted son. He sent him on errands a lot,
paid a little money and gave him a tiny amount of drugs,
sometime for testing product. If you could imagine, Steve
was our nonviolent, unimpressed citizen.

Chapter
11

Deeper
It Goes

"Charley," Julius said to someone on the phone, as the Steve situation still had the floor. "They gonna let you out before they start shipping. I know. I know." Julius was looking our way, clearly listening to both conversations.

"What you bet him Steve," I asked.

"Twenty dollars. The Pacers beat the Bulls, right? But I was wrong. I was goin' pay 'em," Steve said.

"Why you bettin' against Jordan?" I asked.

"The Bulls had it. They about to go down," Rock said.

"About had it? Did you see the score?" Larry asked.

"It was a good bet," Rock said.

"Yeah, ok. What? You told him to bet that shit?" Larry asked.

"The Pacers just beat them two in a roll," Rock said.

Julius was looking concerned while talking to his father. He was talking about Lorton and the fact that DC government had to shut it down. My uncle has been in jail for fifteen years and didn't want to be shipped out. Julius was trying to convince him that he would be coming home before the whole population was shipped out.

"Larry should've gave him the money. He was the only one out there. Know what I'm sayin'?" Ant said to me.

"Eh Steve, when you told dude you was goin' to pay him, what he say?" I asked.

"He said, 'we bet, game over, I want my money, now,'" Steve said.

"And Larry, you couldn't give him the money?" I asked. Larry looked my way and didn't say a word.

"Oh, yo Larry, what kind of games you playing, letting a nigga hit Steve like that?" I said.

I really didn't like the fact that outsiders came to our block and did that to Steve with Larry right there. It was a no-no, plain and simple.

"Shorty, look, like I said, he's a man, like me," he said.

"If Cee Cee didn't come get me, dude would have stomped Steve and Larry," Rock said.

Steve's face was pretty beat up for a twenty dollar bet. I didn't understand why they would do that to Steve. He was the one in the crew that nursed wounded birds. Why would you want to hurt someone like that?

"Lil' L, before you leave, talk to me," Julius said holding the phone to his chest.

"Larry," he continued, "is Mag in our pockets?"

"Nope," Larry said.

With the phone to his ear he said, "Yeah, he right here," and handed me the phone. It was my uncle Charles.

Charles was my mother's brother and Julius's father. He had been in jail most of my life. I went with my mother to see him a couple of times. He was in jail for drugs and weapon charges. My mother said he was the one who took her to the hospital the day I was born.

"Hello," I said.

"Hey, boy!" Charles said, "I been hearing good things about you."

"Oh, yeah?"

"Good things. You stay close to Julius. He say ya'll tryin' to do big things out there."

"A little somethin', somethin'," I said.

"I'll be coming home soon. Hey, tell my sister I love her. I haven't had time to call. A lot of things goin' on down here. Hey, you and Julius need to come see me."

"Ok," I said.

"You just stay close to Julius and I'll be home soon. Hey, make sure you take care of my sister," he said.

It was something about that last sentence. Take care of my mother? Huh? *I'm included now*, I thought. I'm doing okay. My uncle knew this. "And take care of my sister," he had said.

It was my turn to relieve Julius from helping my mother with rent. I didn't know how much he gave her, but I knew he had helped us with a lot. I was the man now.

Later,I had Ant and Rock singing,"Hail to the Redskins" as I smashed both of them in Madden.

Julius and I went to the room. He told me supplies were low and he handed me flyers for his party.

"We had a soda bottle left," I said.

"Larry told me he needs it," Julius said.

"The whole thing?" I asked.

"You and your boys moving fast. Who you dealing wit?" Julius said.

"Dudes from school and folks I met at #11 Boys Club, up Barry Farms and Wahler Place," I said.

"What you think?" he asked.

"Break it up. I got people on hold right now."

"We goin' have to take a ride to re-up."

"Cool, let's go," I said.

"All right, the ride will take two or three days. Tell you what I'm a do. I'll break this up 'tween you two and you'll take the ride to re-up."

"When?" I asked eagerly.

"I'll let you know."

"I gots people on hold," I said.

"You alright lil' cuz, just take your time, and don't spread yourself too thin. People start talking fast, then all hell breaks loose."

"What's up wit the tickets?" I asked.

"Look, I like what you doin'. Just know who you doin' it wit."

"I got you. Me and Ant been thinking about taking our game on this level for a long time. I got you."

"All right. I got seven tickets for you. Do what you want," he said, "but this WKYS party. I want you to party a lot and work a little, know what I mean?"

I shook my head, yeah. He had told us that we would have to pass out flyers, but work wasn't hard, partying was.

Julius gave me eight ounces and Larry the other eight, I was happy. I got the tickets to the biggest party in D.C. since "Go-Go Live." I thought Julius was fair. I didn't have any idea what Larry was up to, going to Julius behind my back. Julius gave me about two thousand flyers.

"Who going to pass out all these flyers," I thought. He told me to go to the HOBO shop, Shooters, ALLDAZ, Ghetto Sports and any other local barber shop or boutiques that we may know. "Networking, we got to network," he said.

Two thousand flyers? Two thousand flyers, come on man, I thought. Didn't say a word though, I was going to find a way.

Larry could have talked to me about the sixteen ounces. We were running from the same source. He could've talked to me. Over and over that came to mind.

He was finding ways to make me mad. I liked Steve, and I really didn't like the Mayor getting beat up. Why Larry stood there, I still didn't understand, but it came to me later.

I asked Julius about getting a car. He said, "Yeah, I'll have Rock or Larry get it for you."

Ant had a fit when I told him. "I told you man," he said. This was just another reason for me to be excited about life, and Julius was the center and source of it all. Thinking back, when my uncle said, "take care of my sister," that was brilliant.

When he said that, I had a fresh thought concerning my mother. I had the means to lessen my mother's burden, and I was going to do just that. My money was all right, so why shouldn't my mother be all right as well. Why should my mother have to suffer because my father misunderstood freedom? My grandfather was on the porch as I approached. He was sitting on a white folding chair listening to Robert Johnson.

"What up, Buck?" I said, as he pulled the cup from his lips. Getting old," he said, taking a pulse. He poured another cup of gin in his elephant glass.

"Ya look good to me," I said.

The night was clear. Stars were easily seen from the porch. The day had turned to night and the dust from the evening commotion had settled down. There granddad took a seat on his porch with his gin. A few people were out and about, and peace had returned as it does now and then.

"Getting old is not for the weak at heart," he said, with an exhausted sigh.

I never thought of him being old. He was just my granddad, but he was in his eighties.

In all respects he was a platinum human being. His eyes had seen a world that tolerated the degeneration of his people as a norm. He had walked in a life that valued skin color over love. He served America in World War II.

He had seen his leaders killed and his neighborhood go from families with doctors and lawyers to pimps and whores.

"How you like the book so far?" he asked

"Don't know," I said.

"Listen, the other books are important, but you must

read, *Soul on Ice* and *Lord Jim*. I will then give you the *Book of Life*, and the *Book of the Horn*," he said.

"Ok," I said.

"It won't hurt to look in a paper. Did you hear about Marion Barry?"

"Yeah," I said, thinking on another level.

"Everybody had jobs and money. He gave it all to the people. The control board did ok too, but it's time for them to go."

At the time, D.C. was under a "congressional seizure." The world said we were out of control, and so, the control board came.

"Yeah, ok," I said. I didn't think about politics all that much.

"Just pay attention. Pay attention, ok? Don't drink too much because it will slow you up."

"Let me tell you, you need knowledge and information and let me tell you another thing, Julius made up his mind; you need to make up yours, all right. I love you just the same."

When I got in the house, I told my mother to wake me up for church. Under her breath, I could hear her as she thanked God for Robin.

Chapter

12

The
Rainbow

Robin and her mother picked me up around 9:30. I put on the dirty bucks Julius brought me, and a pair of black pants with a button-down shirt. Steve and Coleman were outside when I got in the car and started to laugh as we pulled off.

"You look nice, young man," Robin's mother said.

"You don't have a tie?" Robin asked.

"Nope. wrong question," I answered.

"He doesn't need a tie. He looks just fine," her mother said.

"Good morning, beautiful. I don't need a tie," I said.

"Good morning."

"I am here Robin. I am going to church," I said.

"Ms. Wilkinson, my mother said you could come by for dinner later, if you like," I said.

"And this is a day the Lord has made," Ms. Wilkinson said.

I thought she was about to go to church on me. She turned on 1580 and sang along with the praises.

"Are you a member of a church?" Ms. Wilkinson asked.

"I went to Sunday School when I was young," I said.

"That's good." she said, nodding her head.

The church I remember as a child had wooden seats and I didn't understand a lot of the rituals. I remember seeing the preacher, but I don't remember one thing he may have said. I do remember what I was taught in Sunday school and that was, "Jesus loves you," I remember that. I was too busy on the floor, laying on the seats or playing in my mother's lap to hear the Shepard's voice.

The church had beautiful red cushion seats and an organ with pipes that stretched to the ceiling. The women at the door had on white dresses. They greeted us, handed us programs and showed us to a seat.

Service began with prayer and chanting. Then a church clerk read church announcements. The choir sang, "To the Father be all the praises."

As a teenager I didn't notice the fellowship, but I will never forget when the clerk said, "After we tithe and present offerings to our Lord, we will have a selection from our very own youth minister Robin Wilkinson and the very next voice you will hear is that which comes from the Spirit of the Lord."

I looked over and whispered, "Youth minister?" She smiled and on cue got up and walked to the microphone.

I didn't notice her dress until she got up. The black and red dress covered her shoulders and stopped at her knees.

"And they sing the song of Moses the servant of God, and the song of the Lamb, saying...'" Robin began to sing and her voice was sweet as a honey comb.

"Power and honor to you, Father, forever and ever. Thank you Lord. And thank you Robin, what a beautiful voice she has," the preacher said.

You could say that again, I thought, that was my girlfriend.

"There is a story and it's about life," the preacher said.

"You know, I was thinking about the different rules and customs we have."

"Preach on preacher!" someone yelled.

"I was thinking back when I was young, and I used to have those little, what I call, adventure people and animals. I mean, I had them all set up in my little community.

I had the mom, the pops, the basketball court, the boyfriend, the girlfriend, I mean the whole thing. Can I get an amen?" he said looking at the congregation.

"Then my little brother would come in, and mess up the whole set-up, and if it wasn't him, it was my mother. You know when moms clean, they clean, amen.

"And I used to get mad. Why my set-up? Mom had the whole house. My brother had his on toys. But then I would rebuild and restore the whole set. Other times I had to start over, because they messed it up so bad. And that's what the Father did when He called on our daddy, our ancient daddy, Noah."

"Yeah," another yelled.

"It was all messed up, I mean look at it, it's right there in Genesis 6:5. 'Man was great', it says, '...that every imagination of the thoughts of his heart was only evil continually.' But our daddy '...found grace in the eyes of the Lord.' Now, listen up church, it grieved the Lord 'at his heart,'" he said, sternly. 'I will destroy them with the earth,' the Lord said, and He directed our daddy to build the Ark, and the Lord made it rain. He made it rain, and rain, and rain, and rain," the preacher said, pointing his finger, "'All in whose nostrils was the breath of life, of all that was in the dry land, died.' Church, make sure you understand me, DIED! Our Father had to rebuild.

But I tell you, listen to this," he said, rubbing his hands together. "'I do set my bow in the cloud and it shall be for a token of a covenant between me and the earth. My covenant, which is between me and you and every living creature of all flesh; and the waters shall no more become a flood to destroy all flesh,' the Lord said.

"Now, church," he hesitated. "In this new world many nations, like America, Egypt, Germany, Ethiopia, Israel, and China don't agree on much, but they all agree that the earth was flooded. Now, how it happened, many disagree. Some said the sea rose and others said it was an earthquake. I say, The Lord God Almighty, did it. And I thank Him for the Rainbow. Thank Him, church. Remember the Lord when you see the rainbow, and know, He will not flood the earth again, yea!

"Sometimes, He will break you down – ha!', but with your help, He'll rebuild you – ha!' Remember the rainbow – ha!', the rainbow – ha!', Yea!"

I was very quiet and attentive while the preacher gave his sermon. But thoughts of the party came in and out my head. It was a big day.

"What you thinking about?" Robin asked.

"A lot."

"You like my church?"

"It's ok, but I like you more," I whispered.

"Don't say that."

"You my girl. I like you more than your church?"

"Don't say that," she said, like the subject was taboo.

One of the last things the preacher kept repeating, "Go with what you know, start there, and have clarity in your heart."

I didn't know Robin could sing. She didn't tell me they were going to call her to the front.

But when they called her, she stood and graciously walked down the aisle with her hands on her side. When she began to sing, I noticed her movie star pearly white teeth against her pretty black face. Watching her sing praises so effortlessly made me feel warm inside.

I thought the day couldn't have started any better. I just

saw my girl singing like she was Patti Labelle and in a few hours I was headed to the biggest party in D.C.

"You think your mom'll let you go to the party?" I asked Robin.

"I don't want to go," she said.

"It's a show. You'll be back by eleven."

"No, I don't want to go."

As Robin and her mother took me back to the hood, Ant called.

"Yo, you still in church, man?"

"I be there in a minute," I answered.

"Yo, nigga, we ridin!" Ant said.

"The nigga still in church?" someone asked, over Ant's voice. It sounded like Ronald, but I didn't ask.

"We ridin', son! Your peeps be lookin' out. Where ya at? We ridin', son!" Ant said.

"Yeah, who out there?" I asked.

"Rock, Ronald, Larry, Fingers, and Coleman. Yo, Ronald need two and I'm tryin' a wet down before we go."

"I'll be there in a minute," I said.

When they dropped me off, Rock brought me some keys and pointed to a light green four-door Caprice Classic.

"For me?" I asked.

"For us," Ant said.

"Yea, and it ride good, too," Rock said.

"Cool, I'm a take this shit off and see for myself."

I smelt the yams in the hallway, the cinnamon, the syrup and the garlic. Yes, garlic, it was her cure-all. She put it in everything. She was cutting carrots and string beans when I walked in.

"Mom, you goin' crazy wit' the garlic," I said.

"It smells good, huh?" she said, pouring some on the greens.

"It's burin my nose," I said.

"How was church?" she asked.

"Ok. Robin sang today."

"Oh, bless her heart."

My mother had turkey in the oven, cranberry sauce on the table and the whole house smelling like Thanksgiving.

"What up with the big dinner mom?" I asked. "Well a few things, but we didn't have dinner on Easter because of you know who," she said, sarcastically.

I just looked and said, "Mom, I got something for you." I handed her three hundred dollars. She looked and asked, "Where you get this from."

"I earned it," I said, shaking my dice.

"Don't want it," she said.

"I got more. It's just somethin' to help you out."

"I want you to get a damn job, you hear me Larnell?"

"You take Julius' money but you can't take mine."

"Larnell, get the hell out my face. Get the hell out my face!" she said, slamming the pot franticly.

How could she take Julius money and not my money? I thought. I couldn't understand that. What was the difference? Maybe I shouldn't have used the dice, but it all came from the same source — the streets.

While I changed my clothes, I continued to think about it. But couldn't understand, what made her so mad. I tried to do what my father didn't do. I wanted to lighten her load. Take the responsibility from Julius and begin my journey toward manhood.

"See, ya later mom," I said, as she poured cooking grease in a Maxwell coffee can. "You make sure you get back here. Your uncles are coming over."

Chapter

13

Hood
Politics

I walked around the car from trunk to hood. The tires
even looked good. It was a 1989 classic with all the trim,
including a CD player. I named it the "Green Hornet." It
was the perfect day, the perfect weekend and, I had a car.

Ant, Rock, Coleman, Ronald and I set out toward
Pentagon City Mall. I put Rare Essence in the CD deck. Ant
rolled up one. We entered Interstate 295. En route, we
passed the military headquarters of the United States and
the Jefferson Memorial. A monument, "designed to
resemble the Pantheon of Rome." And they were the
furthest things from our minds, as we exhaled ganja's smoke
in the air, talking and laughing.

"Yo Rock, you box or somethin'?" Ant asked, choking.

"Man, puff, puff, pass. Rock you beat him down, huh?"
Coleman said.

"Wait man," Ant said.

"Up number eleven Boys and Girls club," Rock
answered.

"Word? Cause it look like it," Ant said.

We sat in the parking lot and finished two bobs.
Coleman nodded off the smoke. I watched all the pretty

ladies going in the mall. I didn't see a lot of men going in the mall. Just car loads of women. The ratio was something like four to one; women.

"Mag and his crew, them niggas gettin' on my fuckin' nerve," Rock said.

"Yeah, and that nigga that shot that gun, fuck him, too," Ant said.

"Yeah, nigga name Raftin. He flunky, though. We 'bout to go at 'em. Fuck 'em right up off the block."

"Man, I'm wit' it," Ant said, "I never liked them niggas."

"Don't they live around there," Ronald said. "How you gonna say that? Ey, L, we goin' up Solbiato, I need to get this shirt?"

We sat in Pentagon City Mall parking lot. My spirits were high. I thought about getting some Armor All and a couple of Car Freshener trees, a Vanillaroma or a Strawberry.

"Yeah, his name is Magnus and those people in 4200 not his peoples," Rock said.

Rock told us this Hollywood like plot. He said Mag was with a West Indian-New York connection and that they had spots off of MLK, Alabama Avenue and Georgia Avenue. And that Larry was the one doing business with them. They stopped buying from him, but kept hustling on the block. "They want the block," Rock said, "But they did it the right way. Fuck 'em. Yeah, I don't care if they moved in or not. Fuck 'em."

Magnus and his crew did move in, which was better than getting a girlfriend. Having a girlfriend in someone else's hood didn't give you right to sell drugs there, but that's one way to get inside.

It took time for people to warm up to you under those circumstances. But when you move in the hood, the process of acceptance is much faster.

"That's not his sister. She a fuckin' worker," Rock said.

"Who?" I asked.

"Magnus people."

"So, that's not Tony's mother?" I asked.

"We don't know."

"A big show, huh?" Ant said.

"It's a big ass show and I'm about to shut it down," Rock said, "Larry don't believe it though. But he did tell Julius 'bout Magnus' other spots. From the first day I saw 'em I didn't like 'em," Rock said.

"What Julius say?" I asked.

"He told Larry to handle it. Julius tryin' to set up the business. And I say fuck the business! Magnus stop buying from Larry and got them eight niggas on his coat tail."

It sounded like a movie to me, but at the same time, I thought, if those things were true then the game just got serious.

"If I find out Tony is a fake, I'm gonna break him," Ant said. "Ya hear, L? I'm a break that nigga."

"Shorty, don't worry 'bout it. We got this," Rock said.

"Ya'll crazy. When ya'll goin' to get some more water?" Ronald asked.

"Man, fuck that," Ant said.

"We got this, trust me," Rock said.

"Yo, is it that serious?" I asked.

"Man, playin' special agent Hollywood type shit," Rock said, "but the clean-up man is on the way. The show is over."

"Lets invite that nigga Tony to the party," I said, "and work on him."

"Julius say shit like that," Rock said. "Ya'll think alike, huh?"

"Yeah," I said, "but he don't sell drugs. He's cool with us. Let's get him to the party."

"That's too soft. If he wit' that shit, you think he gonna tell us?" Ant said.

"Look, the dude that Don Don killed, you know the one

that was waiting for him at the apartment? Dude was working for Magnus too," Rock said.

"So, Don Don didn't kill his brother?" I asked, chewing a Now and Later.

"No, the dude killed his brother."

The inner workings of hood politics, I thought, used spies like the world's big governments. This seemed too complicated.

Made up like a good Hollywood story.

"Wake that faggot up," I said, talking about Coleman. "Wonder if Steve is goin' to the party?"

"Julius might make him go," Rock said.

"Where he at anyway?" I asked.

"At the Hip-Hop Urban Summit."

"I heard Russell Simmons and P-Diddy supposed to be there," Ronald said.

"All right, calm down," Ant said.

Julius was invited by WKYS to the summit. He was serious about what he called "getting to the right of the streets." But his father, Don Don, and promoting seemed to occupy his mind. The reason we were at the mall was to promote his party.

"I just hope we hurry up and re-up," Ronald said.

"Don't worry its party time," I said.

I grabbed half of the box of flyers. We walked in the Norstorm's entrance. I started passing out flyers right away. The first person I saw was a short white woman. I asked, "Excuse me, do you party?"

"Pardon me?" she said.

"Um, do you have any daughters you could give this to?" I said, showing her the flyer.

"No," she said, increasing her walking pace.

I didn't discriminate. I gave flyers to women with canes. I told them to give them to their daughters, or their daughters' daughter.

"You don't want to miss this," I said.

"What's that?" a woman asked.

"The party of the year, that's all," I said, rolling both pant legs up.

"Rare Essence, huh?" she said.

"That's right. Here, take a few. Give 'em to your friends."

"Yo, I told you Mag and his crew was some shit. Don't ask Tony to go to the party. I might end up punching him in the face. I just don't like them. You think Rock was serious about that shit," Ant said.

"Yeah, but I don't know if it's true. You remember Don Don dressed up like a girl? So anything is possible."

"We got drama cause Rock is on a nut."

"Rock always on a nut. We got to get some money. I am not trippin' but I think we should get that nigga to go to the party and work on him. See what he know. Then, we could tell Julius."

"Naw, man. I don't like them niggas."

We continued to pass out flyers. I reminded Ant that we needed to make money. I didn't want to get involved with the politics. Julius would let us know what we needed to know.

All the players in the show were about ten years older than Ant or I. Just thinking about what Rock said messed up my mood. If it was true, Julius was dealing with a small army. Ant and I didn't sign up for war. We signed up to make money, but if Julius said it's wartime, then it was wartime.

Ronald walked up with two bags and said, "We got to re-up because money is low."

"Hello," I said, answering my phone. "Yo," I said to Ronald, "You gettin' like Ant with the shoppin' an' shit."

"Where you at? We sittin' waiting on you. I thought you was going to bring me the tickets by three," Kim said.

"Soon as I finish, I'll be over there."

"Well, what time is that. Don't nobody have time to be sitting in the house all day waiting on you."

"I'm a get the tickets to you."

"Tell her bring me a girl," Ronald said.

"She might not be goin'," I said.

"What you say?" she asked.

"I was talkin' to Ronald," I said.

"Look at these Aldo joints," Ronald said, pulling the shoe out the box.

I told Kim I'll be there after I finished passing out flyers. I passed out every flyer and didn't give one flyer to a guy.

Maybe it's me, but women are just plain beautiful. As I passed out the flyers, I noticed that all the women were wearing tight jeans and skirts. In my hood young black women always wore tight clothes. You saw their rank and file daily. But now you see European women, Asian women, Indian women all wearing tight clothes. You would break your neck trying to keep up with them. I tried to give each one of them a flyer.

On the way home I dropped flyers at the HOBO Shop, Universal Madness, We 'R' One shop and Ghetto Sports. When we got back in the hood via the Eleventh Street Bridge, I stopped at the Big Chair to meet Kwon.

After I dropped Ronald off, I turned on Alabama Ave. and made a right on Wheeler Rd. At the corner of Varney and Wheeler a tan Impala jumped off the curb and stopped right in front of us. It had lights flashing on its dash.

Squad cars were coming from everywhere. I didn't see them hiding on the creek side. The creek went through our hood for several miles and on each side there was about seventy-five yards of grass and rocks. There are about seven bridges and at this particular bridge on Wheeler Road, they waited for our approach.

"Put your fuckin' hands up," the man yelled.

"What the fuck?" "Oh, shit." "These motherfuckers,"

voices in the car uttered.

"One more fuckin' time, put your hands up!" he demanded, with the gun pointed at me.

When I put my hands up, another officer tried to open the door. With my hands up, I said, "What? What I do?"

"Open the fuckin' door!"

"Oh, man," Coleman said.

I put the car in park and unlocked the doors. The officers quickly opened the doors. One grabbed me and threw me to the ground, put my hands behind my back and cuffed me.

"Where's it at? Just tell me, don't make me look for it," he said.

"Where what at?" I asked.

"Who car is this?"

Before I could answer, "It's Cee Cee Rugil's car," Rock said.

"Did anybody ask you, Rufus?" the officer said.

"Rufus?" I thought. I was glad Rock jumped out there and answered that question. I would have said it was my car.

"What you doing? Where you coming from? Why you with them? You know them bad guys? Where you get this from?" he said pulling out my money.

"Crap game. What I do officer?" I said.

"Got one," an officer yelled.

"Man we ain't do shit!" Ant yelled.

"Fuck boy, if you don't keep your mouth shout. I'm a put something in it," an officer said.

"Y'all always fuckin' wit somebody," Ant said.

"Tell your man to shut the fuck up or I'm going to lock all y'all asses up for drinking and possession. Now shut the fuck up!"

"Y'all some fake ass cops," Ant said.

"Cool out, shorty," Rock said.

"Yeah, tell him Rufus," an officer said.

"Lock all of them up for possession and I get his ass for

disorderly too," an officer said.

"Naw, man!" I said, as the officer picked me up.

"These yours?" an officer asked. He showed me four small packs of crack and a few sacks of PCP.

There were about fifteen officers all around us. A few were standing around while others checked our pockets and went through the car. They were black and white with ponytails and cornrows. They looked like they came from the gym. Mr. Olympian type dudes who were hired by the D.C. government to attack Southeast. This was an extension of the nation's war on drugs.

"Naw!" I said.

"You gonna have to pay," he said.

"Fuck!" Coleman yelled.

They took his shoe strings and put his belt on the Caprice's roof.

He had a zip-lock bag full of crack.

"For real, that's not mine. That's not mine," I said. "Who it belong to?" he said, as he slammed me on the hood.

By this time, my life seemed like it was aging about one year a month. I already cried for Officer Thunderbird and I wasn't about to cry again. They were trying to stop us from going to the party, I thought.

"That ain't mine. For real. What? We got a party to go to tonight. You know that ain't mine," I said.

"So that's not your boys?" he asked about Coleman.

"Look, it ain't mine. I don't know about nobody else," I said.

"It's gonna cost you. No, it's gonna cost all of you. You pay or you go to jail. But your man, he's going to jail," the officer said out loud.

I had eight hundred in my pocket. They charged each of us three hundred dollars a piece. And I was glad. I would have paid the whole eight if I had to. I didn't want to miss the party for nothing. I brushed it off and told Coleman I'll party for him.

After the police assault, Ant and Rock walked home as our block was two blocks away. I dropped the tickets off with Kim and went to the Safeway to pick up soup, eggs and Jimmy Deans for Mrs. Parker. I cleaned the car, Armor-alled the tires and felt good.

Chapter
14

Reasoning
Elders

I parked the car around the corner. I didn't want my mother questioning me. I knew that if my sister or anyone of my uncles saw me, they would tell her. She was already mad about me shaking the dice in her face. I looked at the car one more time before I turned the corner to my building. I wondered how it would look with some nice wheels.

I heard the noise as soon as I got in the building. Loud voices were talking over the Four Tops as they song 'Bernadette.'

"He's going to the Hall of Fame," my grandfather said, as I walk in.

"Hey, boy," my uncle Beenie said.

"What up?" I said.

"Dad, Doug Williams is not going to the Hall of Fame," Uncle Chicago said.

"Hey, dad when you gonna get this Curtis Brothers furniture out of here?" Beenie said.

I saw my uncle Beenie more than my uncle Chicago. Chicago lived in Ford City, Pennsylvania. Beenie lived in

Landover, Maryland. Beenie had on an African hat, a pair of blue jeans and a green polo shirt.

An older man was there holding my sisters hand singing, "'I tell the world you belong to me! I tell the world you the soul of me!'"

"He will get in there," Buck said.

"He don't have the numbers, dad," Chicago said.

Chicago had on a lumberjack shirt and some Rhino boots. He was about six-foot-four and about two hundred and fifty pounds.

"He's a trailblazer," Buck said. My grandfather once called football the Gladiators Chess Game on Wheels.

"Trailblazer? Dad, he needs numbers to get to Canton."

"You talking crazy boy. Canton is full of trailblazers."

"What you up to, boy?" Beenie asked me.

"Big party tonight," I said.

"Don't get caught in those drugs. We at the tail end of one of their greatest schemes. The drugs and the guns," Beenie said, "was for your organs and the death of the black youth.

They almost wiped away a whole generation in California, Washington DC and New York. I'll tell you what. They did it for your organs. They needed the organs. You hear that, Dad?"

I looked at him like he was crazy. We went from saying hello to organs.

"That's my son," Buck said. "He's nuts, but it's my fault."

"Dad, you know like I know. They have been plotting and scheming against us since we met them. You hear about the new evidence on how they plotted to kill Martin Luther King and look how they did Malcolm X."

"Look," Buck said, looking at me, "don't get caught up in that mess. It's like everybody fighting over the little boxes within a box, like the game Monopoly."

"Get caught up!" Beenie said, as I moved to the kitchen.

The food smelled good and I couldn't wait to dig in. The man dancing with my sister name was Lionel. He was my grandfather's friend. He was singing with no teeth.

"I love him," he said, of Buck. Every time he opened his mouth he gave spit showers. I stacked my plate with all my favorites. I had my yams in a bowl and on my plate I had turkey, cranberry sauce, greens, macaroni and cheese. You name it and she put it in the pan on that day.

"Why you cook all this food? Why the party?" I asked.

"Your sister is grown up now," she said.

"Huh?"

"She had her first period," she said joyously.

My whole body froze. My mouth began to salivate. I put my plate down and ran to the bathroom. I gagged twice with the chills. I had no appreciation for the rite of menstruation. As a young man, I didn't care what it meant to a woman or the world. I thought it better that they kept that to themselves.

"You silly boy," my mother said, when I got my plate.

"Beenie, they not going to give us no reparations," Chicago said.

"They got companies right now, who say they benefited directly from the exploitation of black people and the slave trade," Beenie said.

"No reparations, Beenie. It's not going to happen."

"Well, that don't seem like America to me. Every time we drop a bomb on someone, we help build them back up."

"How many handouts do you want?" Chicago asked.

"Handouts! They kill our leaders and bribe our captains. And you know they were bribed. They're all rich now. I mean look, they got new evidence about the government being involved with the killings. This is the fucking land of liberty, right?"

"What are you talking about?" Chicago asked.

"Ok," Buck said, "when you find out people in high

places had something to do with the killings of King and Malcolm, what are you going to do? You gonna write the President or the NAACP? They already know. What you need to do is realize that evil is in the world and it doesn't care about you or your leaders. It has its own course. See, the fight is over the sheep."

"Dad, he gone crazy," Chicago said.

"Oh, they tricky up there now," Lionel said, spitting all over.

"They owe us reparations," Beenie said.

"They owe you respect. But if you don't respect yourself, then why should someone else respect you," Buck said, in his old wise man tone.

"What are we going do with reparations, but give it right back. And that's assuming its monetary. There should be one focus and that's education," Chicago said.

"Look," Buck said, looking my way. "Be regular. Use the bathroom. Be regular. It's an art. What goes in needs to come out. Self! Start with self! I fought for this country and my father was abused by this country and his father worked free for this country. Larnell, beg no man for a damn thing in this country."

"Beg?" Beenie said.

"Yes, Begging. That's all we do. Look, we lost the war so they made us slaves. That's not the first time in history that happened. When people lose wars, they take their women and kill or enslave the men. It would be a good day when one of these so-called black leaders showed a little understanding concerning the world they live in." the old man said.

"This is a war, Dad. They killing us right now," Beenie said.

"They not going to get my son. I be got damn," my mother said.

"Who killing us? We're killing ourselves. Nobody is making those kids pull those triggers." Chicago said.

The conversations they discussed were amazing to me. I sat there and listened. They all agreed that there was a problem. They didn't agree on the problem or a solution to the problem.

Captain Buck was the one who seemed to open up the hidden door of understanding concerning the Africans in America and their situation. The old man was great in the hood. People all over our hood respected him. He was a man willing to die for America and his family. We have had presidents who can't claim as much. With all his knowledge he remained in the hood.

I just wanted to know one thing, who was this 'They,' they always talked about?

"First it was slavery, then Jim Crow, then the gorilla and AIDs, and now the drugs and guns for organs," Beenie said.

My grandfather looked at me again and said, "Don't get caught up in those conspiracies. Be regular. Your uncle is full of it. He needs to take a dump."

"Beenie that kind of talk is holding people back. Its baseless and you can't prove it." Chicago said.

"Yeah, the elephant wounded the dragon and propaganda is necessary," the old man said. "Because people always act off feelings instead of reasoning. I'll tell you what to do."

"Dad, you need to drop the Democratic Party. That's what they need to do," Chicago said.

"For what?" Buck asked.

"They're not doing anything. At least the Republican Party..."

"Look, the Democratic Party adopted Lincoln long ago," Buck interrupted.

"They don't believe in handouts, Dad," Chicago said.

"Only between themselves," Beenie said.

"You ever heard of 'No Interest Like Self-Interest?'" Buck asked. "Black people need to get some self-interest.

We don't recognize and celebrate our freedom. We don't recognize and celebrate our history. We don't have a leader. We don't teach our children our story and you know why?"

"Who want to remember slavery?" Chicago asked.

"We remember Auschwitz, but we don't want to remember slavery," the old man said.

"Dad, its no sense in that. We are Americans now. These kids need to stay in school. Their education can be traded and they need to know that."

"Let me tell you something, son. The whip and the brain have created a very dangerous human. Every white friend I have knows something about himself and his ancestors. I mean look at Tony. You walk in his store and he is reading a Greek newspaper. What do you call a Jewish man, Greek man and English man walking down the street? Huh? You call them white Americans. That's the magic trick. The magic trick is that some Black Americans believe people are just Americans. But these different groups lobby Congress from their interest here and their interest in their grandmothers' land. Like dogs, I tell you, trained with the whip, but that's why I am here," Buck said, looking at me. "You got children in school more then eighteen thousand hours, you hear me, eighteen thousand! From K to the twelfth grade and they are illiterate. My grandson will know relevancy."

"We had education almost as long as we've been free. What of it? They still trick us." Beenie said.

"Our own people are tricking us. Our entertainers have become our leaders and the leaders the entertainers. Look, when you have entertainers talking about the mothers and the fatherless in the poorest communities. And the elected leaders walking right behind them, saying 'Yea, Yea, it's about time someone said it.' You got a trick. They act like they never read, 'Defend the poor and fatherless: do justice to the afflicted and needy.' Don't get me wrong. Ozzie Davis and Jim Brown are certified leaders who speak truth. But some of those other ones don't have a clue and they speak for someone else. Just wish them well," the wise man said.

"Dad, people not thinking about that now," Chicago said.

"We thinking about reparations right now. That's what we thinking. That shit was wrong. They know it. So they should pay," Beenie said.

"Let me tell you. Now listen to me, huh," the old man said. "Reparations, in the grand scheme of things, is nothing. Maybe Cornel West and a few other brilliant people could come together and calculate the total amount of America's slave services and mail the totals to all Black families. Then let the children see how much they are worth. Let the rich of our people and the entertainers pay for the postage, ah. Tell the government to keep its money."

"Now you are talking crazy, Dad. What's that going to do?" Chicago asked.

"It's time to fight for something. I mean, like we forgot," Beenie said.

"Fight? The only thing you need to fight for is the right to your history. Let me say that again. The only thing," he took a pause, "you need to fight for at this point, is the right to your history. Let the children have their history," Buck continued, "It's ok to tell them about George Washington and Thomas Jefferson. These men were great, but slave owners nonetheless. We teach our kids about the brave slave owners who wanted freedom, but not about any brave heroic African kings, who loved life and their neighbor."

"Dad, I, I don't see it. That makes no sense. We are getting it done another way through education," Chicago said.

"That's what I am saying, Chicago. We need the Talented Tenth, something like that, and they need to create an agenda. And let education be the first on the list. Not reparations. How can a kid be in school more than eighteen thousand hours and still be illiterate?"

"That's because that no good ass, evil ass white man. I'm tellin' you. You hear me?" Beenie said, looking my way.

"Anger is not the answer and evil don't have a color," Buck said. "All kind of people share a desire for destruction in the name of self-preservation. You got Black people who don't care about the welfare of Black people. Just open your eyes. It was a Black man who helped the racist kill Emmitt Till, a Black man. And Emmitt was only fourteen years old when they tortured him. Now listen, here is another fight, Beenie. And that is whether or not we are going to be Colored-Europeans or African-Americans. If we chose to be Colored-Europeans, then we do as the Europeans and we are not doing a bad job at it, now. We celebrate almost everything they celebrate. If we choose to be African-American then we must have a better understanding of our ancestors.

"One thing we could at least do is respect their strength. They endured and here we are and," he said, looking directly at me, "Wally called me today."

I haven't met a man in my life like my grandfather. He was one of the greatest men who ever walked this earth. He was the elder who didn't leave. Captain Buck was the reasoning elder who considered the matters of his people and the world.

"They not gettin' my son! They not. He ten minutes from boys school," my mother said, looking at me. "You ten minutes, you hear?"

I sat there and listened like I always did. I never said much. But I did wonder about the "They". Like who was this magical "They" and where did they come from? And who are the 'Talented Tenth' that they could understand my grandfather.

"He's all right, honey," Buck said.

"All right my foot. He around here shaking dice in my face. He 'bout to get a one-way train ticket out of here," she said.

"Shaking dice?" Chicago asked.

"He's all right honey. He needs this community as bad as the community needs him," the old man said.

"It's nothing here," Chicago said.

My mother started telling my uncles what happened earlier.

"He's all right, honey," Buck repeated.

"He needs to be thinking about school," Chicago said. Then looked at me and said, "You plan on going to college?"

"No, he wants to waste himself. But I got something for him," my mother said.

My sister walked over and handed me the phone. And it couldn't have happened at a better time as the conversation turned toward me.

"Here dirty," she said.

"What up?" I said, with the phone to my ear.

"Nigga, you almost ready?" Ant asked.

"Be 'bout thirty minutes. Talkin' to my uncles," I said.

"Yo, we got to get to the barbershop. You know we supposed to meet them niggas at eight."

"A'ight nigga!" I said.

When I hung up the phone, Chicago gave me this ireful look. I looked at him like, huh? And he said, "Don't you ever say that word again!"

"What word?" I asked.

"Nigga," he said, mocking the way I said it. "We don't use that word."

I didn't know what he was talking about. We always used that word.

"That's what I mean, Chicago," Buck interjected. "What is the big fuss over that word?"

"It's degrading," Chicago said

"Says who?" Buck asked.

"Dad, we not niggers, but why Clinton didn't send troops to stop that crap in Rwanda?" Beenie said.

"Of course not, but what is a nigger? That word don't sound no better than the word Negro to me. And I'll tell you why Clinton didn't send troops, because we didn't make him send troops. I'll tell you what Ted Kopple said, 'Once you get people to believe in themselves, that is a force to be reckoned with.' Tell me this, who has done the research among our people about that word? And I will tell you what I mean. The news was talking about the Jonesboro shootings, where those two little boys tripped the school's fire bell and sat outside and played target practice. They killed four little girls and a teacher who shielded another student. That teacher's name was a… a… Shannon Wright. May that teacher be with God forever. Now, when I saw that, I said, those are some crazy little niggers. And, I thought, the word has taken on a life of its own. It's like the word is a non-personal pronoun directed toward men, boys and groups of all races," the old man said.

"Slave owners used that word to degrade us," Chicago said.

"Even with much power, ignorance was a friend, Chicago. The problem is that it reminds some of them of their own ignorance.

Now, we have taken the word right out of their mouths, which is not a real bad thing. That's a sign that we are beginning to define ourselves."

"My children will not use that word!"

"I don't have nothing to say but, give me what you owe me Mr. Christian man. Let Christ be the conscience. I don't have nothing else to say," Beenie said.

"They don't owe us nothing," Buck said, and then looked toward me. "Larnell, they don't owe you nothing. You owe yourself. You owe your mother's mother and her mother and her children. You, just make sure you read those books I gave you and use the bathroom. The Talented Tenth will step up very soon."

"The NAACP is the Talented Tenth, Dad." Chicago said.

"They could be, but the NAACP, has an identity crisis. One, they are not getting to the youth and two, civil rights is their label. See, the NAACP worked on the courts day in and day out. They had to go through the courts to end disenfranchisement and civil injustices. That's why the children must understand that in this country, there were laws to keep us down. See, the youth are not interested in civil rights, but they all should know that the Thirteen Amendment abolished slavery; that's a law. Look, have you ever thought about the visual record of civil rights?

"Martin Luther King led people into a land they were once enslaved in. And in that land they mocked them, hung them, they whipped them and used them. And they marched with no guns! And they said, 'This is our land, too!' While they marched, they were hit upside their heads with bottles and sticks. And you think, how did the Nubians and the Ethiopians end up this way? What an amazing story. But the NAACP have to make its minds up or soon it may have to shut its doors," the old man said.

"Who would it be then, if not NAACP? The NAACP has done good things," Chicago said.

"This group would be master plumbers, doctors, historians, electricians, businessmen, framers, carpenters, preachers and priests. The historians will get the first charge to come up with a book. This book will have uplifting images of people in Africa and America. Once the elders are satisfied, the book will be presented to the government. Simply saying, what has been taken must be returned. Hopefully, this self-awareness would stop you from begging. Now Chicago, there must be self-interest. You must love yourself and then you could love your neighbor. Self-interest! We got to have self-interest as a people. If you think about it, self-interest was the real power behind the slave trade. Self-interest got the laws such that our boys are losing in the name of law."

"The Mann Act was self-interest. Who picks your saints? Think about it; self-interest!" Does Black America have any saints? Why did James Baldwin and Richard Wright die in France? And I'll tell you, the ancient Greeks have the key to an unbiased hidden treasure concerning the Black race. And there needs to be a trip to St. Catherine's Monastery. Never mind they flooded Aswan. The Temple of Beit el-Wali has beautiful examples of own presents. What happened to St. Martin and if a German is white, why an ancient Egyptian isn't Black. Like my father said, the old man continued, "We should thank God for letting us see King Tutankhamun's tomb. …'that it might be fulfilled, which was spoken of the Lord by the prophet, saying, Out of Egypt have I called my son.' Moses was taught in Egypt."

"Larnell," he said, "when you go to work, you think of Egypt. Work like you are building in Egypt. America is your land. Also, beg no man! This is your land. You got off the boat just like they did and it wasn't in the 1900s. Work hard that they may know you by your works. When you go to work, work hard!"

I thought as he looked at me, "I don't have a job."

Chapter
15

Earth's
Heaven

A Glock 26 autoloader was the first gun I received. Julius gave it to me before the party. He mentioned Magnus and told Ant and I to maintain ourselves with protection. One of us should hold the pistol while the other the drugs.

Before we met at the apartment, Ant and I went to All Things In Common barbershop. All the talk was about game seven between Chicago and Indiana. "This is what Jordan lives for, this is what Jordan lives for!" the barbers were saying. They talked numbers, they talked Jordan. The barbers in our hood could sit down with any of today's best sports analysts. But one thing I knew, they didn't know baseball like my grandfather.

I passed out flyers. We got fresh cuts and we went back to the apartment. Ant and I agreed that he would carry the gun while I sold the drugs. I know, why me? Not Ant.

I smelled the ganja and heard the laugher in the hall. Everybody had on Versace, Hugo Boss, Phat Farm, and HOBO. The apartment was packed and Remy Martin was the choice of drink. Ant and I were greeted like young lieutenants.

"Put the glasses up. Now let's get to the right of these streets!" Julius yelled as we drank.

"Yeah," someone returned.

We went outside to pour libations to our fallen. And Julius named about fifteen people and every time he named someone, we poured the Remy.

He even poured one for Frank Sinatra. I poured one for Melvin.

"What you gonna do, Steve?" I asked.

"L, my face hurts, right," Steve said.

"If you stop runnin' into trucks, your face wouldn't look like that," Ant said.

"Right, right. I don't wanna go," Steve said.

"Yes, you do. But you gotta take a bath," I said.

"No, my face hurts," he said as we graded him and took him back up stairs to clean up.

"When the last time you took a bath anyway?" Ant asked.

"The last time your mother took a bath," he said.

"Just hurry up lump, lump," Ant said.

The Mayor got fresh. He put on one of Julius's gold cashmere sport jackets, a button-down blue shirt, blue jeans and some dirty bucks.

"Clean. I mean, Steve, you clean, son. You feel better?" I said.

"My face hurts."

"Hello," I said answering the phone.

"It's time nigga. Where you at? Come on outside," Ronald said.

"We be down in a minute," I said.

We all pulled off at the same time. There were about fifteen cars with our crew.

Ant, Ronald and Steve rode with me. Julius told us to meet him at the super lounge. When we got there, people were everywhere. A line was around the corner going down

Seventh Street.

"Look at this," Ronald said.

"This joint gonna be like that," I said.

And we were ready. Ant had on his dirty bucks with some black Phat Farm jeans, and a shirt he got from We R One. Ronald had on some slick ALDO's and his patent Apple jack hat.

I had on a pair of Kenneth Coles and a pair of Black Hugo Boss with a shirt I got from Ghetto Sports.

As we were going down on the escalator, I felt like my life had reached that moment in *Scarface* when the money started rolling to the bank and he married Elvira. *The World Is Yours*, I thought. Trumpets were blowing! I thought I heard Lil' Benny blowing the horn as we rode the escalator.

I looked down on the crowd and everyone was beautiful. There were women all over the place and the players weren't far behind. Our time had come and, it was like I heard Scarface's *"Push it to the Limit,"*, the song performed by Paul Engemann, playing in my head.

"Push it to the limit, walk along the razors edge, don't look down just keep your head or you're finished, open up the limit! Even the chorus sang; "To the Limit.."

We met up with Moe and Kwon and went into the super lounge. People of all races were mingling. Julius was at the bar talking. Ronald and I stopped in the restroom to take off our under age drinking bands. Then my phone rang.

"Hello?" I said.

"Where you at," Kim asked.

"'Bout to get my drink on," I said.

"Here you go," Rock said, handing me a bottle of Moet.

"Oh… oh, look at her. Hey mommy," Ronald said, to a young lady walking by.

"Hi," she said.

"It's on tonight!" Ronald said.

"Yo, you talk with Julius, 'bout that shit Rock told us?"

Ant asked.

"Naw, my uncles was at the house," I said.

"You got a pen?" Ronald asked a young lady.

"Yo, you need to talk wit' him," Ant said.

"Here you go," she said, giving Ronald the paper.

"Here," he said, handing her a piece of paper, "put your number on it."

"You smooth, boy," I said.

Kim walked in with four girls. One of them had on a pair of leopard pants and they fitted her like tights. Kim had on a red dress that stopped at her knees.

And her toes, what can I say, 'Skittles.'

I didn't get a chance to catch up with Magnus's cousin Tony to see if we could get some information. But I walked over to the bar where Julius was located. I thought maybe he could talk to me more about what's going on. He did give us a gun, so I wanted to know more about what was really up.

When he saw me coming, he pulled me right in. There were about six people around him and three of them were women.

He introduced them all to me and kissed me on the cheek.

"I love you, baby," he said.

"Back at ya," I said.

"Umm," she said, "so you the L?"

She began to get closer and move up on me and it took Kim all of two seconds to get over there.

"Can I talk to you," Kim asked.

"I'll be over there in a minute. I'm takin' care of business right now," I said.

"Ok, but excuse me," she said to the young lady. "Could you not do that."

I sat down beside Julius as he ordered another bottle of Remy Martin. He continued to introduce me to people.

"You got some flyers? Give her some. A classic, you

better come too," he said.

"Hey cuz, what's up?" I asked.

"It's lookin' good right now," he said.

"About the gun, I talked with Rock today. He told us this Hollywood type story. Me and my man wanted to know what's going on. I mean, we wit you," I said.

"Where you think Hollywood get it from. It's on the streets. The real people got the stories, you know," he said.

"Yeah, so New Yorkans and West Indians trying to take our hood?" I said.

"That's been their habit, but I can't say that. Don Don'll be here in a minute," he said.

He did say that he thought the dude who Don Don killed worked for Magnus. And that they were still looking into things. He wanted to be sure because Don Don had bodies (He killed a few people), so it could have been anyone. But all the information right now pointed toward Magnus and his crew.

"Wouldn't Larry know?" I asked.

"Larry thinks people are talkin' and it's not as they say."

"You want me to go at that youngin' Tony?"

"Larry gonna take care of it. You be ready to re-up. We gonna take that trip this week. You got those flyers?"

"Yeah, I got people on hold for that Mazon, you know."

"Hey, I love you youngin'. I like how you do things, always did little cuz.

I got a few more people to introduce you to. I hope you ready for this drop."

"Been ready," I said.

"After I get this production company up and going, we gonna get dump trucks and then the studio," he said.

"Cool," I said.

"Then we gonna dump this drug shit in the river and hold to the right."

I walked around with him and shook hands with some of

D.C.'s old heads. Some of them had gray hair and others didn't. He pointed people out. Told me who was who and where they fit in D.C.'s web of power.

"I went to the summit and that dude KRS ONE is on another level," Julius said. "Dude smart. They talkin' mobilization and getting people to vote and work together. That's why we got to take what we can from these streets and flip it."

As we continued to walk, we ran into Russ Parr and Julius introduced us.

"I'm not this big, I just eat," Russ said, rubbing his stomach. "And somebody put their foot in it; somebody put their foot in it." He walked off. I laughed.

Julius said P-Diddy, Russell Simmons, and rap star personalities were at this summit and that they all recognized there was a problem.

"Did they say anything about the organs?" I asked.

"Naw, they talked about music, but in terms of cause and effect," he said.

"Naw, I mean, never mind," I said.

My uncle Beenie had me thinking and I know my grandfather told me to void what was said, but if any of that stuff was true it could leave you in a state of rage, which is an enemy in itself, Buck had said. "Anger must be controlled."

We ran into Biz Markie and Redman in the back hall. Julius stopped and exchanged a few words with Biz.

"'Bout to get busy in Chocolate City," Biz said, as he walked off.

We entered the VIP room and the well got even deeper. This was the hall of the 'Lifestyles of the Hood's 'Rich and Famous.'

They had dice on the pool table. There were three pool tables in that room and one of them had cards on it. One of them had sticks and balls and the other had my favorite, the twin bones that I liked to throw on stones.

"Oh, yeah," I thought, rubbing my hands.

"I got one for ya," the private DJ said. "Hey, P-Diddy, where you at baby? Huh, I got one, look here. Look, before we put the scratching of New York and its hip-hop world with the drums of D.C. and its hip–hop world together, somebody already done it. I got one for ya."

He started playing, Herbie Hancock's "Rockit." And in that Jazz legend's masterpiece you heard our drums and the scratching. I never heard that song before. But I couldn't believe how perfect the song was for that day.

"What they bettin'," I asked.

"A 'G'," someone answered.

"What! What they dropping on the side?" I asked.

"Five hundred and up," someone answered.

"I got to go get my man," I thought. That money looked good. It had to be about five thousand dollars on that table. This was my type of party. They were betting. They had plenty of money and the women smelled good as my mother's yams. The dudes were walking around with those big chains and the ladies had on silver and diamonds.

When I got back in the lounge I noticed a piano playing, but Ronald and Ant quickly got my attention. They were standing talking with Steve, Kim and her friends.

"Yo, Raw Image just ripped it," Ronald said.

"Word?" I said.

"Yo, what he say?" Ant asked.

"Nigger, they bettin' thousands back there, you hear me? They got women."

"What!" Kim yelled.

"I mean, it's women and men back there. Big cases of the green champagne and the yellow champagne, Hennessey, Remy and they bettin'," I said.

"This just came to me," Ronald said, laughing. "Champ, do you know, I am serious. Do you know you got two first names?" he said to me laughing.

"You Fat Albert on crack, wannabe fake rapper, wit your shit sounding all wack," I said.

"I'm serious man, look. Larnell Kenneth. That's your name, man."

I couldn't do nothing but laugh at him. His mind and mouth ran about a hundred miles an hour.

"Where that joint at?" Ant asked.

"Can I get a drink?" Kim asked.

"Here," I said, giving her a hundred dollar bill. With Julius's connect in the super lounge, we were able to buy drinks. We put orders in with Kim for Heinekens and Remy on the rocks.

I walked over to see the piano player. It was a young woman. She was light in skin complexion and very beautiful. I looked at her and she looked at me. At least, I would like to think she was looking at me. It seemed like she was singing to me. Maybe that's what singers do. But she connected onto me and I onto her. She sang like she understood America's ghetto youth and its troubled men.

They said her name was Keyes. I only snapped out of it when, Ant said, "You know her?"

While we were there nursing our drinks, Kwon came by and said, "I saw M.C. Lyte, Scarface and P-Diddy. They just walkin' around. Hey, look Backyard 'bout to play, too. Y'all niggas always talking about R.E. come on and check out BYB."

P-Diddy and Scarface come to the city a lot and know a lot of people in the hood.

Sean Combs know a lot of people in our town. He went to Howard University. Julius said he was the one who tried to get our music in the mainstream, but the record companies didn't go for it.

Backyard started off as it is customary for most of our bands, with soft tunes and jazz. The band gradually climbed the hill of hip-hop/rock/funk. They sounded good.

"Come on. Hey Sauce," Big G, said. "Hold it now!" Sauce was the conga player.

"It's nineteen ninety-eight; all that fake nigga shit is out, ya hear? The band sang. Pushing to the pocket. "Yea, doin' it, for my city! Hobart!" Big G said, "For D.C., Simple City. Hey Sauce, let it ride!" The band rode a beautiful socket beat.

I was like "Oh, shit." And Kim got closer and we partied. Even Steve partied. Big tall basketball players to young hip-hoppers were grooving to BYB.

And women of all nationalities were getting down. You didn't need much imagination; if they had it, they flaunted it.

"Southside, MLK superstars!" G said, "Southwest 203, — Barryfarms. For my city. Trinidad!" "Hey Kwon, G-Unit! SuperStars! Orlean Orleans, Hobart! — Let the beat, Rock!"

At that moment it seemed like the whole arena had an orgasm.

The scene looked like the painting you see on the opening credits to *Good Times*, where the people were waving their hands and bending in all types of positions, like they were partying till 'six in the morn.'

It took me back to the movie *Roots*. The part when Kunta Kinte went to the woods to get materials to make a drum for his little brother and the slave traders jumped out and captured him. I wanted to yell, to the whole crowd, "If you want to feel that drum, if you can't remember that drum, if you loved that drum. D.C. got it for you. It's scared. It's loved. We haven't forgotten Kunta. We haven't forgotten the drum, D.C.!"

"I'm twisted," Ronald said, as we walked out of the dance hall to the corridor.

"Yo, they lookin' for the Mazon Crazon," Ant said.

"Fellas, fellas," Ronald said, putting his arms around Ant and I. I return and put my arms around him and Ant. Ant did the same thing. We stood there hugged up.

One to another as the sweat from our foreheads merged, Ronald said, "I love you bums."

"Back at cha!" I said.

"What up with the feelings? Don't be huggin' me talkin' bout love. You gettin' strange," Ant said.

"Yo, we got to hurry up and re-up," Ronald said.

"This 'bout to be our city. You ain't know?" Ant said.

"What y'all doing?" a young lady asked.

Ant and Ronald opened up their end of our tri-circle.

"She likes you, yo," I said, to Ant about the young lady who was one of Kim's friends.

"Let me take y'all picture," Kim said.

Before she could take the picture Kwon jumped in and there. We were Ant on my right and Ronald on my left. Kwon was in the middle kneeling down, flipping the bird. I looked at the camera with both hands up about as high as my chin and thought, "What!"

From taking a few pictures with Kim, we ended up at the picture booth where we took about twenty-five pictures with friends and different crews from the city. These pictures would have twenty or so people in them, falling over one another, laughing and joking.

"Yo, see if you could get me a tape?" I asked Kwon.

"Yeah, I told ya son. BYB like that," he said.

He did tell me about Backyard Band, but I had no clue they were so good.

I was a Rare Essence (RE) fan. And no one gave it to us like the Inner City Groovers. But thank God for Chuck Brown and his influence.

"Look at that nigga," Rock said, pointing toward Larry.

"Julius said Larry got shit under control," I said.

"Larry a fuckin' liar," Rock said.

"What you talkin' about?" I asked.

"Why everybody know what's happening except his ass," Rock said.

"Know what, yo," Ant asked.

"What Magnus is up to," Rock said.

"You at the party. Hey mommy, come here mommy," Ronald said.

"Man, she 'bout two hundred fifty pounds. What ya gonna do with that?" Ant asked.

"The best lovin', boy," Ronald said walking toward the young woman.

The stars were walking around with ease. They didn't put on airs. It was as if we were celebrating a wedding. I saw Donnie Simpson and the WPGC family, Fat Joe, Nas and when RE performed Ludacris and Redman did a song with them. And even the human beat box, Doug E Fresh, came and did about five songs with RE. Kwon went to get me a PA tape.

And I hoped they had one for their new fan.

"Julius said meet here after Essence play. We ridin' to Ocean City tonight," Rock said.

"Cool," I said.

"Don Don back," Steve said.

"Where he at?" I said.

"Yo, that nigga Don Don is crazy. Was you there when he dressed up like girl?" Ant said, talking to Rock and Steve.

"Look, at that nigga," Rock said.

"Chill son," Ant said.

"He could have gave me the money, right L?" the Mayor said.

"Yea, but Larry a little strange, Steve. You know him better than me."

"I know that nigger know somethin'," Rock said.

"What you say?" Don Don said as he walked up.

I was shocked to see him. My eyes almost popped out my

head. Ant looked at me and I looked at him. I wondered how he got out. He had two dead people in his apartment and his rap sheet was eight and half by fifty.

"That nigga Larry playing fifty. He know what Mag and his crew is up to," Rock said.

"What you gonna do if he do?" Don Don asked.

"When you get out?" I asked.

"This morning. Your uncle said get down Lorton. Where JP at?" he said.

"In the VIP," Steve said.

"What happened to you this time?" Don Don asked Steve.

"Fightin'," he said.

"You got your ass whipped," Rock said.

I walked off thinking of Kim and whether I could get her to go with me to Ocean City. As I walked though the crowd, she found me. I got close and her Bijon smelled like candy, so I kissed her and held her. "You look good, I mean real good," I said.

"I do?"

"Real good."

"So what you gonna do about it?" she asked, smiling.

"Make a move out of town tonight. You tryin' to roll?"

"Can Sharmain go? She likes Ant, too," she said.

"We'll see," I said.

I saw Larry at the bar and thought there was no time better than the present to get in his head about Mag. He was at the bar doing shots with two dudes. When he saw me he told the bartender, "One more round. One more. Hey L, take a shot to big things, big people and big places." We drank. When he put his shot glass down he said, "Act like a soldier when you go re-up."

"Always," I said.

"Your little youngin' nice. I didn't know ya had it in ya," he said, talking about Kim. *It was the couch*, I thought.

"The couch," I said.

"You messed up my flow. I had shit to do, but it's all good."

"You could have given Steve that money," I said.

"I had it, but the crack head that he is, he need to stop bullshittin' and get his own. He'll fuck it up for people."

"Steve cool," I said.

"Yo, youngin' you movin' too fast. What? You givin' that shit away?"

"What!"

This is why I don't like him sometimes. He talked to Ant and me like little boys. See, he hadn't heard we were about to take the city.

"Y'all youngin' not movin' that shit that fast," he said.

"Shit movin' itself. What? You got a problem with me," I asked.

"Back down, shorty. If I had a problem, I would have told ya."

"So, what up with Mag and his crew? They fuckin' with Steve an' shit. That's some bullshit!"

"Get out your feelings about the crack head. Steve is a fuckin' crack head," he said.

"Naw, it's about Julius. What kind of game they playin'? I asked.

"Shorty, back down. Don't let that little money go to your head."

"Man, that's my cousin!"

"Yeah, and that's my main man. Mag is playin' by the rules, shorty. I got this and if we slip, we slip."

"Ain't no motherfuckin' slippin'! What that mean?"

"Don't let that shit go to your head," he said, as he walked off.

Chapter
16

18 Seconds

Ant and I sat in the car with Kim and Sharmain waiting on Julius's caravan to start to Ocean city. Ronald left with his big love doll. Ant was at the wheel and Kim and I were sitting in the back.

I never been to a better party in my life.

The caravan took off toward New York Avenue. We were about seven cars deep as we merged onto route 50. Julius said we were going to meet a New York crew and continue our party.

"I think I saw Jay-Z," Sharmain said.

"Man, I saw so many people. And I passed out all my flyers," I said.

"You didn't see no damn Jay-Z," Ant said.

"How you know?" Kim said, resting her head on my shoulders.

"How you know what?" I said.

"He said…"

"What you talkin' bout? Go to sleep," I said.

We continued to East on route 50. I was drifting in and out while Ant drove. As I continued to do so, I noticed the cars in front of us disappeared.

"Where the fuck they go?" I asked.

"They act like they racin' and shit."

I drifted. And out of nowhere the brakes screeched and the car slid to the right. Kim and I almost ended up in the front seats when we stopped.

Good thing Sharmain had on her seat belt or she would have been through the window.

"What the fuck!" I said.

"I saw something."

"What the fuck did you see?"

"Damn Ant," Kim said.

"That nigga too high. You want me to drive?" Sharmain said.

"I thought I saw a tractor trailer flipped over," Ant said.

"What!"

"For real, I thought the shit was on its side."

I got out and checked to see what it was Ant saw. And I didn't see a thing. Not even a dead squirrel.

I checked the car and took the wheel. I called Julius and he said stay the course.

"Man, damn, I am telling you, I saw something."

"You saw that motherfuckin' Mazon. You been smokin' that shit?" I asked.

"Man, I need to roll one," he said.

"You don't need nothing else," Sharmain said.

"Did I ask you? Hey yo, what that nigga Larry talkin' 'bout," Ant asked.

"Some jealous type shit," I said.

"Yo, I wonder do Don Don know they wanted to kill him. Cause he sure don't act like it."

"It's like fighting for a box within a box. Julius know, fuck it," I said.

I didn't want to talk about too much with the women in the car. All that Hollywood type business was serious and I didn't want to talk about stuff I didn't know about.

"I fucks with that nigga," Ant said.

"My uncle... hey, check this shit out. My uncle said that they created AIDS, put the shit in a lab, and shit. And now it's killin' our ass. And the fighting over the drugs and guns is actually for our organs," I said.

"Yep, yep!" Sharmain said.

"Man, stay away from faggots. Look, y'all just stay away from some of those faggot motherfuckers who want to get fucked in the ass and then go to a club and find a girl," Ant said.

"They didn't create AIDS," Sharmain said.

"I don't want to hear that shit, my brother died because a nigga don't know what he wanna be," he said.

As we approached Ocean City we drove to the north end of the city. I called Julius and told him our location. He told us to meet them further up north, near the Delaware boarder.

After we dropped the girls off, we met them. And everybody had guns. Even Cee Cee had a gun. It was about four in the morning as we walked on the beach.

And Rock just unloaded a Uzi, dropped a clipped and reloaded.

"Make fire!" Larry said.

They all were in the water to about their chins.

"You ready?" Julius said.

Ant went first, then me. And it was a rush I will never forget. Firing toward Africa and England, dropping empty clips and reloading was like New Year's night in the city, but we were on the beach, in Ocean City. I unloaded two clips in eighteen seconds and it felt good.

I went back to my room. And as Kim was taking off her clothes I thought, "What more can I want."

I believed that Southeast had everything one could dream for. It had money; it had women and its own music. I was living life better at this time than my mother and she was working as long as thirteen years. Men who were fifty weren't even living like us. We were betting thousands in craps and in pool halls. I had my own car. I walked in and out of VIP rooms giving daps to some of Black America's underground superstars and to its hip-hop stars.

Kim was standing before me with a see-though bra and matching thongs. To me, life couldn't get any better. *This is the life*, I thought. She came closer and I kissed her and rubbed her. And yes, she was soft as cotton and smooth as a baby bottom.

Then the phone rang and it was Julius.

"You talk to your mother?"

"Earlier."

"You didn't give her your number yet?"

"Man, mom's crazy. I couldn't do that."

"L, man, call your mother and give her your number."

At that moment it was like Kim turned into a big black ape. My mood went straight to the trash can. I called her.

"Who told you, you could stay out? Who the hell do you think you are, Larnell?"

"I'm wit Julius."

"I don't give a good got damn who you with. You get your ass home now!"

"Mom, mom, I'm all right. I'm seventeen years old."

"You ain't seventeen yet. You can't even fuckin' pee straight and you.. Look, get your black ass home. Larnell, I am tired of this. I'm tired."

"Mom, I can't. We 'bout two hours away."

"I'm tired of this shit, you hear me?"

I was exhausted when we hung up. I told myself that I wasn't going to tell her about the car or the phone, but I did. I put my clothes back on and went on the balcony to smoke a bob.

Chapter

17

A Reason
for War

We left Ocean City after game six between the Bulls and Pacers. We watched Jordan and the Bulls pull it out again. When I got in the house, my mother told me I was punished. I didn't know what to think of it. But I didn't go back outside that night either. I talked to Robin and went to sleep.

The next day in school, while in English class, I asked for a pass to the restroom. The subject in English was 'modifying compounds.' I really didn't get the stuff they were teaching us. *What is that*? I thought. Modifying compounds, it wasn't relevant to me. So I thought it was better that I modified my situation.

And I did. I went straight to the bathroom. Went in a stall and sat on the water tank with my feet on the seat. I stayed there until it was time for my history class. I sold five ten packs and tried to get a crap game going. Ronald finally showed up.

"I need like four bottles today, man" Ronald said.

"Straight. This my last day. I'm not comin' to school tomorrow. You seen Ant?"

"No."

I never once thought about how China was training their children or India for that matter. I didn't think about school as a vehicle to knowledge or the fact that knowledge comes from information and its information that gives you understanding. And it's that understanding that will allow you to build a foundation. I never once thought any of that while in high school. Maybe I was being trained to be a working class guy. No real purpose, just a worker. I didn't know what the Department of Education's objective was concerning my generation. They called us YXZ or something like that. Maybe their objective did work or maybe it didn't, but what I do know, a lot of people dropped out of school. There was one class that I didn't want to miss. And I didn't.

When I walked in class, Mr. B was sitting at his desk.

"What up, Mr. B," I said.

"How are you, Larnell?"

"Cool."

When the class settled down for lessons, Mr. Binshem, stated, "The 'Hutchinson letters affair' was a blessing in disguise as the Colonies were in the process of taking up arms against England. Franklin's effectiveness in England was damaged as a result of the Hutchinson's matter so he prepared to come back to America. At that time, events in America had turned for the worst."

"The Tea Act of 1773 and the Intolerable Acts of 1774 were two of the last Acts of Parliament that completely turned America against England."

Those events followed the Stamp Act and the Boston Massacre, events that put the relationship on shaky ground. Mr. Binshem said the Colonies had had it with England, which resulted to open rebellion.

A lot of the hostilities were due to Parliament imposing taxes on the Colonies. England needed revenue to offset expenses received from the war with France and the Indians. The way in which Parliament went about it caused the rebellion.

I wanted to make sure I heard him correctly so I asked, "Mr. B, is you sayin' the War of Independence was because of taxes?"

"There was a little more to it, but basically, yes."

I couldn't believe it. But he went on to say that shortly after Franklin got back to America, he was appointed leader of a committee to meet with a representative of Great Britain for the purpose of Peace, but as 'free and independent States,' something Great Britain would not consider.

"They met, they talked, they parted. And now nothing remains but to fight it out,'" Mr. Binshem said.

Thus Franklin went to France. In France he was a star. He was already known throughout Europe for taming lighting, his work with electricity and his writings. In his services for America, he got guns, ammunition, clothing and some twenty-six million francs.

He was also in charge of the naval activities and had John Paul Jones raid English ports and towns, something England did not expect. I was amazed at all Benjamin Franklin had done for humanity and America.

My grandfather once said, "If you give your dog credit, then you could give a human credit as well."

"Benjamin Franklin is the essence of America in its beauty and glory," Mr. Binshem said. "Here we have a man who didn't graduate from any college, but he started one. Here we have a man who let his Black servants go more than a hundred years before Lincoln signed the Emancipation Proclamation.

Here we have a man who invented the rod that catches the hand of fire. The author of Poor Richards Almanac and the diplomat who secured the resources that helped America win its Independence."

As Mr. B talked I thought about when I turn on lights and listen to the radio in my car. Not to mention PlayStation and the ground wire. Through Benjamin Franklin's research and discoveries we have a better life. Now, when you throw in what he did for the Revolutionary War, the result is a great human whether he is black, white or red.

"I want you to think of America as Benjamin Franklin did, as a land of possibilities. Here, you don't have to be close to a King. What you need to do is imagine and have the will to do.

I once told my wife that it was in the soil. Because so many of the world's greatest people and inventions came from America. It got to be in the soil. It must be in the fruits and vegetables, I told her.

People like Thomas Edison, Madam C.J. Walker, Henry Ford and Russell Simmons and Wilbur and Orville Wright. These people are Americans, but their efforts have changed the entire world," Mr. Binshem said.

After class, Ronald and I went to the hood. It was a nice sunny day. I went to Sam's to get the car washed and make a drop with Met at the pool hall.

"Joe, y'all was shooting for real?" Ronald asked.

"What I say, man? Where you and the big girl go?"

"To do the damn thing, nigga. You know how I roll. Did Ant get some?"

"He said he did."

"Was that a real platinum chain Met had on?

"I guess," I said.

"Man, niggas are crazy. I asked this nigga up G-town one day what is the difference between platinum and gold. He told me it was the color and the bubbles. And you know what those bubbles are?"

"What?" I said.

"Vegetable oil!"

"Met didn't have bubbles on his chain."

"Naw, it's when they're workin' wit it. See, its like they get silver and they cook it in vegetable oil. And the bubbles in shit, those them bubbles when you cookin' chicken and shit. Man, that's how they make platinum, man. And they got these niggas out here, like they found the next best thing to a big ass."

"You funny," I said.

The phone rang.

"Hello," I said.

"Hey." said Kim.

"You miss me?" I asked

"Yes, where you at?"

"Me and Ronald headed back around the way."

"Mama want you," she said, handing her grandmother the phone.

"Honey," her grandmother said, in her golden voice, "Honey, I need a favor."

"Ok," I said.

"I need eighty-five dollars for some food and medicine, baby. Do you have it?" By this time Kim and I was pretty close and her grandmother knew I had money coming in loads.

We dropped off the money and pulled up on the block. Ant, Wembo, Cee Cee, Rock and Julius was there.

"Big girl lover," Ant said to Ronald.

"Best loving in the world. Try some," Ronald said.

"What? You dropped out?" I asked Ant.

"Man, school over. Fuck school. Nigga tryin' to make that money."

"You need school, dummy," Cee Cee said.

"You had some dude hanging all over you at the party,"

Ronald said to Cee Cee.

"Don't say nothing else to me, Cee Cee," Ant said.

"Yea, that was my husband," she said. "He mad now."

"I didn't see you dance with nobody but him," Ronald said.

"I went to Ocean City. He didn't like that."

"I didn't know you were married. You crazy," I said.

"I take care of him," she said.

We sat there and reminisced about the party. Talked about our party and whether or not, we were going to have a good crowd. Julius was talking to Rock. Wembo was off to himself.

"Yo, give me them four joints so I can roll," Ronald said.

"Straight. Let me holla at Julius and I will get that and some flyers for you," I said.

Me, Ronald and Cee Cee walked over to Julius and Rock.

"What up, cuz?"

"Cee Cee punished," he said.

"That nigga gonna beat her ass," Rock said.

"Shiiiit," Cee Cee said.

A black Impala pulled up slowly as we were talking. And before Rock could say, "Who is that," the front door opened and a man jumped out firing with what looked like an Uzi.

And then all you heard was, pop pow! Pow dow! Pow! Pow! Rock ran to counter. Julius got low. The sound of glass and people was falling to the ground.

"Watch out!" someone yelled. Ronald jumped on Cee Cee and they fell to the ground. Wembo opened fire on the car.

Pop! Pop! Pop! Pop! Pow dow!

Semi-Automatic weapons demanded respect and destroyed at will as the strength of the cowards had increased a hundred fold. It was a good thing our hood had the steel equalizer on ready.

I watched Julius as my heart ponded a hundred miles an hour. And he reminded me of Colonel Kilgore in the movie *Apocalypse Now*. While bullets were flying around he was busy using the two-way pager saying, "Black Impala, black Impala." I didn't see any fear in him. He was the true leader in the heat of battle, directing people to the enemies and their black Impala. I looked at the car spinning off in haste and back toward Julius. He roused up and walked toward Wembo.

Wembo had blood on his shirt. I got up and brushed the dirt off my face as it was packed like shaving cream. When the Impala left our block, the windows were blown out and bullet holes riddled the side.

"Shit, I got one," Wembo said. "I got one."

"Where ya hit?" Julius asked Wembo.

"Don't know. I got one of them motherfuckers."

"Julius!" Cee Cee yelled.

I looked and saw blood. Cee Cee was scooting from under Ronald. I shook my head, hoping that my eyes were tricking me. Ronald was lying on the ground in pain and shock.

"Shorty hit bad. Call the ambulance," Rock said.

"Ronald?" Ant called out. "Ronald."

No response.

I kneeled down with Ronald. The blood was coming from his torso. He gritted his teeth and shook his head.

"You gonna have to fuckin' get up, champ," I said, moving his bloodied white tee.

"You can't move him, L. Put pressure on the hole," someone yelled.

As he was shaking, I saw his eyes roll to back of his head.

"You can't die on me," I said.

"Hold the spot, shorty. Hold the spot," someone yelled.

"You can't fuckin' die on me. You hear! Hold on nigga! Don't fuckin' die," I said, holding tight, with tears rolling down my face.

"Hold on nigga, don't fuckin' die on me."

He just kept shaking. And I just held on to him. I couldn't hear a voice. I held him and talked to him. I begged him to stand and rise like a soldier. I held him until he shook no more. I held him. I held my friend in my arms, his blood and all.

Chapter
18

The
Meeting

The 'Fast Life' course took on another meaning on that day. Every week and month I was in the trade, I felt I was getting older and older. But that day, as I sat in Julius's car, covered with blood, the course was near completion.

"Why the fuck he not gettin' up? Where we going," I asked Rock, while he helped me in the car.

"Police comin'. We got to get the fuck out of here," Rock said.

"The ambulance is comin' for him. Cee Cee and Fingers is gonna stay with him," Julius said.

I couldn't get myself to together. I was in a vertigo state. I felt like I wanted to throw up. I had my forehead in my palm and my elbows on my knees, just shaking my head.

"Look, just tell them, I know, I know. Just tell them what you know. I need you to focus. Cee Cee! Listen, just tell them, ok he saved you. I know, just tell... Look, I need you to call Bro, ask him about hospitals and tell him it was a black Impala. I need to find out who they were and... Ok, he saved you, I know. If you can't do this, have Fingers do it by himself."

"That's some fucked up shit!" Ant said.

"Can we stop? Where we going?" I asked

"Where is Larry ass? That motherfucker! He knew I knew he did Julius. You got to stop believing that motherfucker?" Rock said.

"Larry went up the Players Lounge to make a move. Look, we gonna let shit calm down," Julius said.

"Calm down? Pull over, fuck calm down. You hear! These... man I..! I yelled. "Did Ronald just die? Fuck calm down."

"The ambulance got him. He'll be ok," Rock said.

"Man, fuck you. Did you see him, huh? Did you? I'm gonna throw up in this fuckin' car. Can you pull over?"

"No, just throw up," Julius said.

Julius kept driving. It all seemed like a dream; life with all its fun and laugher is maintained by blood.

All I saw was blood. I didn't hear Ronald make a sound. I saw the shaking and his eyes, but I didn't hear a sound. If I was happy go lucky, now I was lucky and very unhappy.

"Y'all still got that shit on ya? That's why we on the road, now. Think. When they pull up and see blood on you, you would've been locked up with 'possession with attempt to distribute.' You got to think, you hear? I know that's your man. We gonna let shit calm down and go back to see him. But you fuckin' got to think or you might as well shoot yourself in the fuckin' head."

We got on interstate 270. I just kept my head down. I thought, as soon as I get a chance, I was going to run up in that apartment. All I knew was that my buddy was on the ground and I didn't give a good got damn about the rest of that shit.

"That nigga Larry know something, Julius," Rock said.

"Know what?" Julius asked.

"Niggas been talkin' 'bout this kind of shit going down. Larry is the fuckin' one who was supposed to keep them in check. Now look. They come through and Larry no where to be found. He went to make a move. Fuck a move. That nigga know something," Rock said.

"Look, Wembo said he got one. So whoever they are, we'll find out real soon. Fingers and Cee Cee gonna let us know real soon," Julius said.

"Did they call, yet?" I asked.

"Man, that's some fucked up shit, when you find out somethin'. Me and my man gonna take care of it," Ant said.

"We ridin' tonight. Roll that shit up," I said.

Me, Rock and Ant smoked two blunts. The weed seemed to calm me down a little. I took my gun from Ant on the way. He said it jammed on him. We still hadn't heard from Cee Cee or Fingers by the time we approached Mind and Body. I didn't have to sit on the purple chairs this time.

They rushed us straight, though. Mimi was waiting for me. She looked uneasy as she took my hand. It looked like she had tears in her eyes. Like she wanted to say something but didn't know what to say.

"I need some tea," I said.

"Yes," she said.

I wanted to believe that I was in a dream and it wasn't so. What I did know, when Ant and I found out who did the drive-by, we were going to handle it ourselves. Mimi came with the tea and I drank it like a shot of Remy.

"Get me another one."

"Me no can do."

"I don't fuckin' want to hear that shit. Get me another one."

"Take shirt off," she said.

"I'm not takin' my fuckin' shirt off. What the fuck you talkin'"bout? My man just got shot, ya hear?"

She walked out. I sat down on the couch. The room had one table, one chair, the couch and a counter full of oils. I felt myself relaxing a little. But every time I closed my eyes,

I saw Ronald shaking. She returned with another tea. And I drank it in a rush, like a cool glass of water on a hot day. She sat down and watched me, and what seemed like a moment later, I watched her take my shirt and lay me on the table.

It's in the tea! The shaking I saw when I closed my eyes gave way to bright lights. The lights were spinning faster than Arance-Monaco spinners at a red light.

I drifted further into dreamland. I felt like I was still on the table, but the wind blew forty miles an hour. I held on tight as it blew.

"Relax," I heard a voice say. "Be like water, adapt." And when they said that, I felt the table no more.

The lights numbered twelve. They began to travel around me at the same velocity they did when they were at a distance. These lights uttered in different tongues, one after another, and sometimes together. While I was with the wind and the spinning stars, my hands were clean and my t-shirt didn't have blood on it.

When the wind and lights stopped, I was sitting in a reception area with nice contemporary furniture. I didn't recognize anything or anyone. My t-shirt was bloody again. I touched my back and the Glock was still there.

"Would you like to clean up before the meeting?" the woman at the desk asked.

"Do it look like it?" I said.

"Sir, you could clean up," she said.

I got up out the chair and went to the receptionist desk and asked, "Who in the fuck is you? My fuckin' friend just got shot and you talking 'bout cleanin' up. Where the fuckin' meetin' at?"

"Sir, he will be with you in a minute."

"What is this?" I asked, looking around.

The place had marble floors and counter tops, big pictures and its conference rooms had glass walls.

"We'll seat you now, sir."

The conference room table was made of granite. A picture of Tiger Woods was on the wall. A black gentleman walked in with clean blue suit. You could see the gold cufflinks under the coat sleeve. He was clean shaven, no mustache.

"We have white t-shirts, son. It would be best for you to clean yourself," he said. I just looked at him.

"No, really. We must maintain respect for the décor," he said.

"Respect for the décor? What about the blood on my shirt?"

"What can I do for you, son?"

"We need help," I said.

"You don't know how to read?"

"Yeah, I know how to read. I'm talkin' bout the hood."

"Can you speak Spanish?"

"Look, man, my fuckin' friend just got shot, and all you can do is sit there with your fuckin' legs crossed talkin' 'bout Spanish. How many Indo-European languages we gonna have to learn?"

"I'm talking about the future, son. Let's have some respect here."

"Respect? Respect what?"

"I understand your friend has been shot. But what can I do for you?"

"He was just standing there and 'em m... just started shooting!" I said.

"Did you call the police?"

"For what?"

"What can I do for you?" he repeated.

"Are you one of those 'talented tenth' of the people? Is this your place?" I asked.

"Yes," he said.

I didn't know to which question the answer came. But it didn't matter; a yes was all I needed.

"We are asking for your help. Talk to the other Black elites and tell them we want to be free. We need your help!"

"Wait a minute," he said, putting his hand up. "You are free."

"No, mentally free," I said. "We want to be mentally free."

"Mentally free? What kind of talk is that?"

"History has a funny way of repeating itself. Why is it we don't celebrate our freedom? Every nation of people I look at celebrates their release from bondage, except the African-American, don't you find that amazing?"

He leaned back in his chair and with his pointer and thumb rubbed his chin and said, "What do you mean?"

"My friend just got shot. I know you didn't do it, but this type of stuff happens all the time. We don't have enough fathers in our neighborhood. Half of them are dead or in jail."

"There are new programs in the works. We are not going to leave no child behind," he said.

I didn't know what he meant by that. Maybe it was that sound bite, hands-off kind of talk. I thought my purpose in the meeting was because I was a youth from the inner city.

But I also knew that I was a messenger sharing ideas given to me by my grandfather and the twelve lights.

"Have you ever heard of the Junto?" I asked.

"No, I haven't, but keep in mind programs are coming that will help the inner cities. But you need to remember that no one can take your education away from you," he said.

"Listen you take this back to your people. If they think victory has been won, very well. But I am here to tell you, we need help. We need the 'talented tenth' of our people to create an organization whose sole interest is America and its African-American interest. We want to learn about ourselves. We appreciate the other races, but it's about time we appreciate and respect our ancestors."

"We do. We fought for King's holiday," he said.

"Yes, and King died for us and who stepped in his place?"

"What are you asking? Where are you from?"

"The Lawless Goldmine," I answered. "Have you heard *'And the Lord said, like as my servant Isaiah hath walked naked and barefoot three years for sign and wonder upon Egypt and upon Ethiopia; so shall the king Assyria lead away the Egyptian prisoners, and the Ethiopian captives, young and old, naked and barefoot, even with their buttocks uncovered, to the shame of Egypt.'* You know they called Jack Johnson an Ethiopian."

"What does that have to do with why you are here?"

My anger roused instantly when he said that. I couldn't believe what I was hearing from this man who has benefited from the sacrifice of others.

"Do you cry, sir," I asked, "for the blood of Malcolm X? Do you cry for Dr. King's life or wonder what life would be like if they didn't cut the leaders off from their people? Do you? Huh, do you?"

Then MiMi appeared. She rubbed my shoulders intensely, saying, "Walk like a champion, talk like a champion."

We were like the Fourth Dynasty Egyptian Prince Rahotep and his wife Nofret sitting there. "Walk like a champion, talk like a champion," she kept saying.

"Listen to me, son. I want to help you. What can I do?" he asked.

"Talk to your people and tell them to lobby Congress and work with the Black Caucus. We want our history. It is written the poor shall be with us always, but why should we be physically and mentally poor? Why should we have no money and no self-esteem? Why? Let me remind you, as Robert B. Edgerton did, '...European and American scholars neglected most aspects of African history, dismissing African culture as well as Africans themselves as inferior.

African religions were discounted as pagan, their customs as barbaric, their governments as despotic, their architectural achievements as nonexistent, and their minds as, well, to be charitable, more like those of children than adults. As recently as 1963, Hugh Trevor-Roper, the Regius Professor of Modern History at Oxford University, wrote: "Perhaps in the future, there will be some African history... But at present there is none; there is only the history of Europeans in Africa. The rest is darkness... and darkness is not a subject of history. That kind of dismal and arrogant ethnocentrism has been rendered laughable by anthropological and historical research.' Laughable, you hear? Laughable, but is it? The last time I checked, they still don't feed the new seeds their proper nutrient."

He just looked at me, shook his head and said, "Who are you?"

"I'm the grandson of Captain George T., the son of Willard S., the son of Daniel, the son of Oba, taken by hekaw-khasut ('the chiefs of foreign lands'). I'm the son of Ahmose, the son of Seti, the son of Piankhy from the land of Punt behind the gates of Meroe. That's who I am, sir. And another thing," I said. "Do you remember when the high priest's servant came after Jesus and Peter drew the sword and cut off his ear? Huh, do you? Well, you tell your friends to stop talking about our mothers.

You see," I said, taking out the Glock and putting it on the table. "We have these and AK 47s now and let them know that our mothers are still with us. So, if they don't have anything good to say about the women who are trying to hold us together while our fathers are in jail, dead or running around like a bunch of clowns with cufflinks, then don't say anything at all. And remember what Jesus said, I continued, '...*I am the root and the off-spring of David, and the bright and morning star.*'

If the Lord Jesus being the example of the new world

speaks of roots and history, then his followers could do the
same."

◆　◆　◆　◆　◆

I felt like I had a very strange dream, but I couldn't
remember anything but the wind blowing. My body felt
better, but my head was still woozy. I heard Rock's voice first
as I approached the South East room.

"Motherfuck what you talkin' 'bout nigga. I didn't know
shit. How the fuck that sound? Fuck you!" Larry said to
Rock.

"Everybody know what's going on. Niggas been talkin'
'bout this for weeks and the day they come through, you not
there. You deal wit' them niggas. So what the fuck is up?"
Rock asked.

Julius was sitting on the table with his arms folded. Steve
was sitting down at the table, while Rock and Larry were
pacing the floor, screaming.

"L, you all right, right?" Steve asked.

"Not really. What that say about Ronald?" I asked.

Steve looked at me and shook his head and I saw it in his
eyes. "He dead," he said.

"What!"

"He didn't make it, shorty," Julius said.

"What the fuck you talkin' 'bout, Julius?"

"L, you all right, right?" the Mayor said.

"I'm ready to go," I said.

"Shorty, you got to chill," Larry said.

"Man, fuck you, Larry, you bitch ass motherfucker. Fuck
that. I'm ready, blood for blood," I said.

"Cool out, L," Julius said.

"Cool out? That was my fuckin' friend. Somebody
gettin' fucked up. I don't want to hear that shit," I said with
tears streaming down my face.

"L, you all right, right?" the Mayor repeated.

"How you know they did it?" Larry said.

"Did they call you back yet?" Rock asked.

"Man, look, what room Ant in? I am ready to go," I said.

"Look, Lil' L, you got to cool out. Your man saved Cee Cee," Julius said.

"What! We supposed to let them get away with this?" I asked.

"Two of 'em got hemmed up before they got away. One dead," Julius said.

I didn't want to hear what Julius was saying. I didn't understand why he was talking the way he was talking. Magnus wasn't in the car so I thought we still had a problem. I didn't want Magnus and his crew to think it was that easy. All I wanted Julius to do was take me home. Our crew would handle the rest. But Julius had another idea.

"Julius, dude just copped from me. He said he didn't have nothin' to do wit' that Don Don shit. Mag said he didn't have no beef," Larry said.

"Larry, we got a problem. Our block in fucked up. Lil' L man is dead. We'll find out in a minute. Fingers got three IDs," Julius said.

When Ant came through the door, Julius said, "We gonna take the trip a little early. Since the block is hot, we'll let things cool down. Me, Lil' L, Wembo and Fingers gonna take the trip to re-up. Larry, deal with Mag. Tell him to stay off my fuckin' block. Tell him to stay off my block!"

"You expect me to tell him that?" Larry said.

"I'll tell 'em," Rock said.

"Larry will deal with him. Ant, I don't want no trouble," Julius said.

"I'm all right," Ant said.

Ant was surprisingly under control considering all that had gone on.

Leaving to re-up wasn't something I wanted to do. I

wanted to find out who killed my friend and pay them a visit.

When I talked with my mother, she was out of her mind, screaming and yelling. "I had enough. I had enough," she said.

Julius told her he was going to take me away for a couple of days. He said she screamed at him too and that she was going to blame him if something happened to me. I gave Ant our car keys.

After Wembo got there, we took off. The first stop was Ronald's house. We put together an envelope for Ronald's mother.

When we got to his house, people were all over. They were on the porch, sitting on the curve and in the doorway. They spoke, grunted and gnawed.

"What happened, Larnell? What happened?" I heard as soon as I walked in.

"That's him?" another yelled!

"Is Miss Brooks here?" I asked.

"What happened, Larnell?"

"They just came by and started shooting," I said. "They just started shooting."

"Who was it?" an older man asked.

"I don't know. I don't know," I said, shaking my head. "But I'm gonna find out."

"What did he say?"

"He didn't say nothin'. He just... he just was bleedin'. Can someone give this to Miss Brooks? They not gettin' away with that. They not gettin' away with that," I said.

"That's right. Get 'em, Larnell," someone yelled.

"They gonna get 'em," another said.

These are some of the attitudes we had in the hood. This existence was more akin to the Wild West than any civilized world order. The normal order in this type of situation would be to wait for the police and then tell them what you know. But the police wasn't very helpful in our world.

We stopped at the spirits store, grabbed a couple bottles of Remy and some Backwoods. I drank a shot and put my head down. The thoughts of Ronald laying there flashed in and out. I got dizzy and felt very nasty.

"I don't want to hear that shit!" I said.

"It'll be all right, soldier," Wembo said.

"Where the bottle at?" I said.

"Larnell, pull it together," Julius said.

"Why we leavin'?" I said.

Julius looked at me and didn't say a word. He put Frankie Beverly and Maze in the CD player and turned it up.

"I got one shorty. He's gone. They won't try it again," Wembo said.

I was in between depression and violent rages. But when I smoked a ganja-filled Backwood, it calmed me down and I fell into a conscience car sleep.

While I was asleep, I heard Fingers tell Julius, after he and Cee Cee found out what hospital the dudes were in, that someone named Tonya gave him the property bag, that's how he got the first ID.

Then he said he bumped a dude that was running his mouth and got his wallet, and he took a pocketbook. Thus be his name, Fingers. I remained in the conscience sleep for the whole ride. I only woke up at rest stops.

Ten hours later, we were in Atlanta and we dropped Wembo and Fingers off at a truck rental. Then he showed me where Martin Luther King, Jr. lived and where he was buried. Then we pulled into Zoo Atlanta's parking lot. He brought a bag of pistachios and we walked.

"You all right?" he asked.

I shrugged my shoulders and said, "You re-up down here?"

"Just a break. I like Atlanta. I get good feelings about the town. This is King's hometown, so stop and make a move. We got a few more hours to go."

"I don't understand why we had to go. It seems like we runnin' or somthin'."

"Have you ever heard of Bumpy Johnson, Queenie St. Clair or Lucky Luciano?"

"I don't get it. Why we didn't go at them niggas?"

"You got to use your head," he said pointing to his temple. "See things through. This is a war and you can't engage every battle as the main event, know what I am sayin'? Wembo killed one of those dudes. It was a shootout. The police are all over and you want to go lookin' for somebody? Who you lookin' for? You got to use your head."

"Magnus and his crew did it. Why you don't see that?"

"Maybe so, but we still got to use our heads. These things happen. Know what I mean? See, now it's our move."

"What's up with Larry? Everybody on the streets is talkin' and he actin' stupid," I said, as we walked in the Ford African Rain Forest. This forest simulated the gorilla's home in Africa. We sat in the area that featured a gorilla named Willie B and his mates.

"This is the real reason I come," Julius said, opening a pistachio.

"What? To look at apes?"

"You got to watch them. That's Willie B. watch him. This is what we'd be doin' if we wasn't so smart. That's Kudzoo. That's his first born."

An ape came over to the window with a stick in her mouth and was gesturing and blowing kisses. This was nothing like the Zoo in D.C.; our apes had a small, outdoor area.

And if you wanted to see them up close, you had to go to the ape house and watch them in the cage. This habitat in Atlanta was different. It was as if we were in the cages.

Julius and I were sitting in this big exhibit hall with enormous windows looking out at gorillas. They had land, trees and physical matter that looked like their home in Africa.

"Things are simple here," Julius said. "You could think things out in here."

"What are we goin' to do with Larry?" I asked.

"Larry is good peoples. He don't mean no ill. He my man," Julius said.

"Your man fuckin' shit up," I said.

"You got different types in the hood, know what I mean? Look at it like this, Mag and his crew live around our way.

We made some good money off 'em. Larry is very loyal. I just don't see.. Look, look that's Machi and her son Willie B., Jr. he one now," Julius said, throwing the pistachio shells in the trash.

Julius was amazed with Willie B. and his family. As time went by, I found myself listening just as hard when he spoke of the apes as when he did about our situation in the hood.

"They said they in a lot of hoods," I said.

"We in a lot of hoods. But you got to think, that's the most important thing. You got to think. Look, you got all kinds of shit against you. It's not like it was when Ray was out. A lot of niggas are hungry. Some dudes in the hood don't care about their own mother. Why would they care about you? Listen to me, you got soldiers like Don Don who is loyal and very deadly. When you get in the car with people like him, you sit in the back. Don't let dudes like that sit behind you. Then you got those get-wits, see they are true followers and do things to get a reputation, know what I mean? You got guys like Lil' South, now both his mother and father on crack. He walkin' around straight layin' people down. But some dudes just want to make money and take care of their families. But we all in the same pot. So, if not Magnus, it would be someone else. That's why you man up, stay ready and prepare yourself to move to the right. But you must use your head."

"Hello?" I said, answering my phone.

"You all right?" Robin asked.

"What up," I said.

"I am just worried about you," she said.

"I'm ok. They just started shooting."

"When are you coming back?"

"I think my cousin took me out of town, just so I wouldn't rip D.C. up."

"Good," she said. "Stop thinking like that. I love you. You hear me? I'm praying for his family and you."

"Ok."

We sat there for about three hours, watching the gorillas and talking, and it seemed to slow my mind down. I wasn't thinking about destroying everything anymore. I just wanted to go back to the hood.

I felt like we ran. If we could have just shown our faces they would have known we stand our ground. We left the park and met Fingers and Wembo at the hotel. We checked in a Holiday Inn and went to the mall.

Julius said they were going to a party later that evening. I didn't feel like going to no party, so I asked them to pick me up a PlayStation, which I played for three days while in Atlanta.

I talked with Ant and he told me that the National Guard was on our block. I also spoke with Robin, Kwon, Kim and my little sister several times while in Atlanta.

On the fourth day, we got up and drove further south. We ended up in New Orleans and went straight to Bourbon Street. The clouds were so low it seemed like I could have touched them. They were much lower than the ones we get in Washington.

Julius got out the car and made a phone call, then went to talk to Wembo and Fingers, who were behind us in the cargo van.

We walked Bourbon Street and about an hour later Julius got the call. We all got in the cargo van and went to a wet, spongy land. That's right, to me it looked like a swamp. There were three dudes outside of the barn-like building. Julius grabbed the briefcase and told me to be on ready. I click-clacked and we went in.

The whole deal went very fast. Julius handed them the briefcase and as they counted, Wembo and Fingers loaded the truck with twenty-six kilos of cocaine and fourteen gallons of PCP.

"It crunk?" the dude said.

"For sure," Julius said.

"West Coast like La La," another said.

"Good deal," Julius said. "Y'all need to come up north a little."

"It crunk?"

"That all depend on what you mean," Julius said.

"Hustla, you could take ya hand out your pockets," a dude said to me.

"Just keepin' it fair," I said.

Julius introduced us and told me this was the Los Angeles-New Orleans connection. After the re-up, we went straight north. It took us fifteen hours to get back to D.C.

Chapter
19

Mom's Wail

Ant picked me up the morning of the funeral. Ant, Kwon and I went outside after we viewed the body. People went in and out. Mr. Binshem came with about six other teachers from Ballou. My mother stayed with Miss Brooks. Ant and I stayed outside until the wake was over, then we went in for the services.

As the services went along Miss Brooks cried more and more. It got louder and louder.

"I am tired of our mothers crying over there baby boys. I am tired of it. I ask you Lord Jesus bless these mothers, as only you know their burden," the preacher said.

"Get up. God.. Why? Oh why? Get up, Noooo… No, no, no," Miss Brooks said.

My mother was with her crying and holding her when she could.

"Why lord? Why? I want my boy. Get up, Ronald. Mommy said get up. Oh my God, no. No, no!" she screamed, as if terror had overpowered her.

My mother was crying just as loud as Ronald's mother. The crying started to travel like the rain coming down the street, headed your way. After a while it reached you.

It began to sound like the whole church was crying. If they weren't crying for Ronald, they were crying for his mother. I couldn't take it. I got the keys from Ant and left the funeral. I sat in the car and banged on the steering wheel for a while and cried in my own peace. I went to the liquor store and bought seven bottles of Remy.

I sat there and poured out all seven bottles in libation for Ronald, Melvin, Don Don's brother, Biggie Smalls, Foots, Tupac, the Heavy One and all the hood's fallen.

Chapter

20

The
Kidnapping

Later on that day, Kwon, Ant and I were sitting in the car drinking in front of Kenny and Paul's Barbershop. I told them about Atlanta and New Orleans. We talked about getting t-shirts with Ronald's picture and passing them out to all our friends. We talked about looking after his mother and making sure we were always on the ready.

My mother called.

"Hello," I said.

"Where are you?" my mother asked.

"Sittin,' talkin' with Ant and 'em."

"I want you to come home now!"

"I'm ok, mom."

"I want my son to come home."

"I'll be there."

"I don't want my son out there. You don't need to be out there. Come home," she said, with her voice cracking.

"Mom, I'll be there as soon as I finish."

"You been gone all week. I want my baby to come home. You hear me? I want you to come home."

We sat there about an hour more. I told them about the

load we brought back from New Orleans and what Fingers and Cee Cee had done.

"Is JP still having the party next week?" Ant asked.

"Yeah."

"We gonna have to get Larry. I mean fuck him up," Ant said.

"So, what he gonna do 'bout them niggas up the way?" Kwon said.

"Don't know yet. He figure Wembo killed one so it's kinda even," I said. After we smoked a Bob, I went in the house. My mother was in her room and my sister was at the table talking on the phone.

"What up, Pooh?" I said.

"Can I have some money? Now, he want a come home, girl. Thank you," she said. "Now you want a come home."

I had no idea what that was all about. I looked in on my mother to say hi.

She was in her room signing some papers. She looked up at me and said, "Did you go by to see Miss Brooks?"

"Naw."

"Don't go back out there," she said, shaking her head.

"I'm tired," I said.

"I can't take it, you hear me? I can't take it."

I went to my room and laid down on the floor. I watched a little TV, talked with Kim and Robin, then went to sleep.

I heard a door shut.

Then I heard what sounded like dog feet and claws, then heavy breathing and whispers.

The door opened and a voice said, "Get up!"

It felt like a possible dreamland situation, as I was in a state of subconsciousness. Then the dog barked and a man said, "Get your ass up."

This wasn't dreamland. The rottweiler barked and leaped at me. It was my uncle Chicago and his dog looked bigger than a grizzly. He pulled on the dog and told him to sit. In an instant, the dog sat.

"What?" I said.

"We are going on a trip," he said.

"What?"

"Get your shit."

"Man, I'm not going nowhere," I said.

"I'm only going to ask you one more time, get your shit!"

"You not talkin' to me," I said.

He walked over and grabbed me. I tried to get loose but before I could do so he started choking me. I couldn't move or breathe. My uncle Chicago was big like a NFL linebacker. My mind was telling him to, "get the hell off me." He was choking me so hard that I couldn't make an audible sound. He took my ego and smashed it with a sledgehammer. He was ten times stronger than Officer Thunderbird.

There I was, Little L, a Champ, I was moving up in the underground, partying with superstars, going in and out of VIP rooms, pool halls, and I had a network so good the old heads took notice. I was stacking my own money, and I had my own car and the prettiest young women in Southeast as my friends. I was a part of a crew that had no problem with war, death and killings, but that meant nothing as my uncle just came and shut me down like a car with no battery.

I said nothing because I couldn't. He took my air and speech. "What the fuck?" I thought.

"Chicago, put him down!" Buck said.

"I can't take it, dad. I can't," my mother said. "He's not even thinking about his sister. I am tired."

"Get out of here, Chicago," Buck demanded.

"Tell him to get his stuff together. He wants to be a man, does he?" Chicago said.

When my mother and Uncle Chicago walked out of my room, I looked at my grandfather, still gasping for air.

He looked at me and said, "Pack a bag."

"Came home," I managed to whisper. I couldn't get the word 'just' out my mouth.

"Look at me. I am sorry about your friend. But there is nothing you could do. Pack a bag. Listen, pack what you need and what you want. I don't care what you put in it, but get it ready. Your mother is going to have a nervous breakdown. Do this. Chicago is not going to let you out of here."

"Man," I said, shaking my head, "What? Go where?"

"Pack a good bag. Put a book in it and whatever else you need."

"I don't wanna go. I don't wanna go," I said.

"Then Larnell, you got to fight Chicago. That's the only way."

"What do she want me to do?"

"Leave," he said.

It was an ego-crushing night. At that moment I realized, in the clearest way, I still lived with my mother. No matter my neighborhood connections, I still lived with my mother, yet I was stacking a small fortune.

"Leave?" I said.

"Your mother is having attacks, maybe some kind of anxiety or something. Just for a few weeks, Larnell. She will be calling you back. Just pack a good bag," Buck said.

He walked out the room and I started packing. I grabbed three white t-shirts, a pair of jeans, a quarter pound of ganja and the book *Like Lions They Fought*. I also called Ant and Kwon and told them what was going on.

"They not getting my son," my mother said.

"He needs to take responsibility for himself," Chicago said.

"They not getting my got damn son. They not getting my son," she repeated.

"Honey, it's ok," Buck said.

"They bring it over here and it's killing these boys. They

not getting my son. All he talk about is Julius. What about his sister?" she said.

"Mom, what you want me to do, cause I don't want to go. I mean, I mean... I just got back," I said.

"And you just about to go. You got your stuff together? Don't say a word about your sister. What about your sister? If something happens to you, what is she going to do?"

My sister? I thought.

"I'll destroy his whole made-up world. He thinks he's a man does he? Let's go," Chicago said.

As we were leaving out the door, my grandfather said, "Listen, if you have a problem with using the bathroom, mix some orange juice and milk together. Now, warm it up, you hear?"

Chapter
21

The
Mountain

My uncle asked me to sit in the back seat. He had a green Yukon. I did exactly what he asked me to do. I felt like I was going to jail. We ended up on Interstate 270.

Oh, shit, I thought, *He's about to go to 'Mind and Body' and destroy everything.* But he kept going. We passed the Mason-Dixon Line, and I just watched the rolling hills and beautiful landscape of Pennsylvania. I saw a sign that said Gettysburg.

Some people have said that it was the battle of Gettysburg that turned the Civil War in the Union's favor. It wasn't until later that I understood 'Key Stone State,' the words you see on Pennsylvania's car tags. A "Key Stone" state it is.

Just imagine if General Lee would have won and driven a wedge between the Union army. Black America would still be in some form of slavery. The United States would look something like the old world with different states and rules and possibly continued fighting. But look at America today, united as, the United States of America. Now, even the South is happy about the outcome of the Civil War.

We stopped at Breezewood and at that time I realized

why he had asked me to sit in the back. He had engaged the child lock on both doors. We went to the restroom, ate and were back on the road.

We were traveling through the Appalachian mountains via the Pennsylvania Turnpike. Southeast got hills with good views and vantage points, but they didn't make your ears pop. We were driving along with the camels and elephants of today; Big Mack trucks, Volvo trucks and international trucks. There were trucks everywhere. They seem to own the road, driving faster than the cars on the narrow turns in the mountain.

He got off the turnpike and went through more towns, one of which was called Apollo. We ended up in a town called Ford City.

The sign said, it was founded in 1887 by a John B. Ford. When we got to his house he said, "We don't use the word nigger around here."

I still didn't say a word. He showed me to the room. The room looked damp and dark. It had a twin cot with a dresser and a lamp. I put my bag in the closet and my phone rang.

"Yo, what you do? When you coming back?" Ant asked.

"I fuckin' don't know. In a couple of weeks, I guess."

"I got that from JP," he said.

"Cool, just bury my money in the ground. I told Kwon and 'em to hit you up."

"Where you at?"

"Up in the mountains, a place called Ford City. Nigga tried to choke me, man."

"Word? What happened? Why moms do that?"

"She talkin' 'bout Julius, saying they not going to get me. I guess Ronald and that whole thing with the National Guard, man. I don't know."

"Damn."

Later while sitting on the porch I received calls and made calls, maintaining what business I could. I noticed a lot of white people walking and driving up and down the road. I even saw a good number of Black people. The houses were small, double-attached units.

The house across from my uncle's house was adjacent to an alley and there was a car there with its hood up. The car was red and it looked like a racing vehicle.

"Come in here. You hungry?" Chicago said.

We sat down and ate. He made some beans and turkey stew. Up until then, he did most of the talking. I didn't have much to say to him.

"What you going to do with yourself?" he asked.

"I am trying to get paid. Julius talkin' 'bout buyin' a truck company and runnin' a production company."

"Julius? He's going to be like his father, in jail, and it could be worst. You can't look to Julius for nothing but trouble."

"What's wrong with a production company?"

"The only production Julius has is drugs, and you know what drugs gonna to do for you? They are going to send you to jail or get you killed. Your friend just got killed. You don't think that will happen to you?"

"We was just standing out there."

"Why would you be standing around people selling drugs?"

"How long I got to stay up here?"

"You need to talk to your mother about that."

I called my mother, but she wouldn't talk with me. But I found out what my sister meant when she said, "Now he want to come home." She knew my mother was setting me up.

Over the next few days my routine was the same. I got up, ate, made calls and received calls.

I went to the porch and read my book. After I read a few chapters, I would take a ganja break. I would go by the old PPG plant and smoke. The plant seemed to be stretched about length of the whole town.

Ford City was a little different than my hood. It didn't have a liquor store or a Chinese joint on every corner. They didn't have a hood like I was used to. I didn't see more than three or four people outside together at once. In my hood we could have twenty to forty people just hanging out.

When I was walking through the alley, returning from my ganja break, the neighbor asked, "You got that good shit?"

"Who you talkin' to?"

This was the neighbor who lived across the street. He worked on cars in the alley. The first day I got there, he had that red racing car in the alley.

"You," he said, "Every time you come pass me, I smell it. So, you got it. Can I buy a nick or smoke one with you?"

I sat there and smoked one with him. He said his name was W.E. and it stood for Walking Eagle. He looked like Brad Pitt with a young lion's mane. I nicknamed him Brad Pittsburgh.

"Most people call me Eagle," he said.

We talked about four-stroke engines, 450 horses and different piston-types.

He talked about cars, parts and how to make them faster, like Ant and I talked about drugs, sports and PlayStation. I told him I was from D.C. and his eyes just lit up. It was as if I was a star just because I was from D.C.

"What is going on with the President?" he asked.

"He got some head and they don't like it," I said.

"What about your mayor, smoking crack and all? The news always talking about D.C."

"Barry ain't scared to come to the hood though. Hey, yo y'all got a Wal-Mart around here?" I said.

Eagle took me to the Wal-Mart and I got 'Madden' and 'Smuggler's Run.' When I got back to the house I found out my uncle didn't have a TV with a video/audio plug.

It didn't matter as much when Ant called and told me he sold two soda bottles. I just told him to "bury my money."

When my uncle came in he said, "Tomorrow, you are going up to the high school to take a test."

"What high school?"

"Ford City High," he said.

"Why I'm takin' a test?"

"You are not going to sit up here and do nothing. And you are going to find a part-time job. We may have some work for you on our road crew," he said.

My uncle worked for a highway road crew. Picking up the road and putting it back down. He said by the time they laid one stretch of road, there was another waiting to be picked up.

He was crazy. *I didn't come up here for that*, I thought. I felt like I was in some kind of Twilight Zone. I was making more money than my mother. I hoped to buy her a nice place with the money I was making. I thought they sent me up there to get away from the block and the National Guard. Nobody told me about going to a new school.

"Yo, I'm headed up Georgetown, do you want me to get you something," Ant asked when I answered my phone.

"Get me the fuck up out of here. They talkin' 'bout school and shit."

"Word? They just messin' wit you."

"I'm going to call my mother and see what she talkin' 'bout 'cause I'm going to find out how to get back to D.C."

"Yo, chill man. Everythin' is everythin'. You just be mad that you gonna miss this party. I'm sellin' more tickets than sacks right now."

"I don't feel like a party anyway. If I was Julius, I would've cancel that joint," I said.

"For what?" Ant said.

"We just buried our man. Fuck partying. I am tryin' get up out these mountains."

"You'll be back in a couple of weeks."

"That's what I thought," I said.

"Julius goin' meet that dude Mag sometime after the party. That's what Steve told me, but you know how crack head is," Ant said.

"Word? Steve know what he talkin' about. When, what day after the party?" I asked.

"I don't know, find out from Julius."

"Word. Tell Steve to call me or somethin' and don't let him smoke no more of that Mazon Crazon. Hey, yo, I think I'm gonna drop Caesar and go with the Zulus. They got heart for real, man," I said.

"I'm goin' with First Street and the Mazon Crazon. I don't know them people you talkin' 'bout," Ant said.

We laughed.

The next day I walked up Fourth Avenue to Ford City High. While walking, I talked with Julius and he told me they switched up the holding spot.

"Things goin' good? Y'all pushin' that Mazon, huh? You just remember what I told you, a little rest don't hurt. We thought about comin' to get you, but your mom ain't goin' for it right now."

When I got to the school, they sat me in a room and I took the placement test.

They didn't time me so I took my time. I stayed there for three hours and after the test I walked back to the house. I smoked a Backwood, got my book and I sat on the porch. Eagle came over and asked, "You want to get a hoagie."

"What's a hoagie?" I asked.

"You haven't been to the hoagie shop yet?" he said.

We went to Miller's hoagie and bought two hoagies. A hoagie was a big cold cut sandwich with the special hoagie sauce.

I almost finished my sandwich by the time we reached Rosston Boat Launch, and we sat there watching the waters of the Allegheny and got high.

"Are you trying to go to Kittanning?" Eagle asked.

"Naw, I'm tryin' to get to D.C."

"I can't go to D.C." he said, "but Kittanning got some action."

All I could think about was going home. I missed my hood. I missed my friends, so, I called my mother.

"Pooh, where mom at?" I asked my sister.

"She don't want to talk with you," she said.

"Man, put mom on the phone, man," I said.

When she got on the phone, I asked her how long did she want me to stay up there.

"As long as it takes," she said.

"For what?" I said.

"You are not doing anything. I told you to get a job. Did you do it? No. Have you seen your latest report card? No. You don't even care about your sister. What if something happens to me? All you can think about is Julius. As long as it takes, you hear? As long as it takes."

"I'll get a job when I get back," I said.

"You are not coming back no time soon. I'll talk to you later, Larnell," she said, and hung up.

That Saturday my uncle took me out to eat. We walked to Odessa's restaurant, as you could walk everywhere in Ford City, which was a few miles long and a few miles wide.

Some of the buildings look like they were from the old frontier. They were very small, two- and three-story buildings.

"Mrs. Ethal, this is my nephew Larnell from D.C.," Chicago said, as he walked to the counter.

"How are you, young man?" she asked.

"Ok."

"You here for some R&R?" she asked.

I didn't know what R&R meant at that time, but my uncle answered, "His mother sent him up here. He doesn't know what to do in D.C."

"Well, we know he ain't the only one," she said.

"Where is Martha?" he asked.

"In the back," she said.

My uncle ordered some Bar-B-Q pig feet and I ordered some chicken.

"Got a call from the school today," he said.

"Yeah?"

"As you know, Ballou failed you."

"I had passing grades."

"No you didn't. You had to know that. You can't pass with grades like that. But the good news is Ford City said they may skip you to the twelvth grade because of your test scores. Now that says a lot about you."

I know he don't think I was going to school up there. He had to be out of his mind, I thought. I was going to find a way get back to my hood. I missed my hood.

"What you need is to get yourself focused, and realize that education is the answer. You can't do anything without education. What Julius is doing has no future and you have to see that," he said, as Mrs. Martha came over and handed him a bottle of Odessa's Famous BBQ sauce.

She began to talk about how she and Miss Ethal shot a pig. "Right in the head," Ethal said. She described how they boiled it, shaved it and gutted it.

Then she said, "That chicken you eating was a feisty one. When I finally caught him I tried to break his neck three times." They could have picked a better time to tell us about gutting pigs and breaking chicken necks. But what amazed me was that these women were Black and that they were full of love and straight talk, and they lived up in the mountains of Pennsylvania.

Chapter
22

Justice and
Judgment

Eagle and I was riding around in his Ford Bronco listening to Nas and Mob Deep. We stopped at a few bars and corner stores. In every one of them there was a pool table. Their bars and corner stores are like D.C.'s convenient stores. You could find one every few blocks.

Then a song came on I will never forget. It was a song by Bob Marley called Concrete Jungle. At this time in my life, I knew hip-hop had a universal appeal, but I never heard 'Concrete Jungle' and Eagle was singing the lyrics like it was his song and he was a white boy and there I was the *black* boy feeling like Bob was singing about my hood, but didn't know one lyric.

"Let me hear that again," I said. I had that weird yet proud feeling I got when Mr. Binshem was telling me about Frederick Douglass. It is very weird when people of other races consistently know more about your people than you do.

"He was the truth!" Eagle said. "You know he took care of thousands of people? He was the truth, man. But listen to this one," he said, as he inserted Bob Marley's Rastaman

Vibration CD into the CD deck. My phone rung.

"They killed 'em. They killed 'em, shit! They fuckin'…" Ant said, with his voice cracking.

"Yo, what you talkin' 'bout?"

"All hell breaking loose, man. They killed Julius and Larry!"

"What the fuck you talkin' 'bout," I said.

"They shot 'em up. They went to meet and they shot 'em up. They fuckin' shot 'em up, L."

"I…," I screamed. "I'm on my way."

"What happened?" Eagle asked.

I told him and he said, "I'll take you back." We made a few stops and left Ford City. My phone started to ring.

"L, it's bad. Oh my God, oh my God," Cee Cee shrieked.

"I know. I'm on my way. What hospital is he in?" I said.

At this point I had no anger. I was mad, steaming mad. But my anger was under control.

I felt like it was my responsibility to torch everything with Magnus's name on it. I've seen so much death that I was numb and totally confused. If you like a good cowboy story, then you would need to go no further than my hood.

Listening to tunes by Bob Marley like 'Roots, Rock, Reggae' where he said, "Play I on the R&B, want all my people to see…" and songs like "Who The Cap Fit," where he said, "Some will hate you, pretend they love you, now. Then behind they try to eliminate you…"

When I got back to D.C., the first place I went was D.C. General Hospital and found that Julius was still living and in surgery, but that Larry had died. We pulled up in the hood and Don Don was the first to move toward me. I stepped back, grabbed and cocked.

"Hold… hold it, L. It's me Don Don."

"Yeah, I know. Don't walk up on me like that."

"Your uncle wants you to come down Lorton," Don Don said.

When I walked into the apartment, the first thing I heard was, "Who's the white boy?"

"His name is Brad Pittsburgh," I said.

"Pittsburgh?" Ant said.

"Yeah, he a team player. Got me out the mountains. Where Rock and Steve at?" I asked.

"Steve been missing in action and Rock is on a nut right now," Cee Cee said.

"Where he at though?" I asked.

"He won't answer his phone," Cee Cee said.

"Magnus is mine. I'm gonna fuckin' kill that motherfucker. Lil' L, don't worry. I gonna fuckin' kill that bastard!" Don Don said.

We sat down and tried to figure it all out. Don Don made it clear he was going after Magnus. Wembo, Cee Cee, Fingers and Ant began telling me what happened and how we should deal with it. It was like the "God Father" when Michael went behind closed doors. There wasn't a lot of emotion, but tears were on everybody's faces. They said that Larry set it all up, but his plan back fired and they killed him, too.

"One of the dudes, we know where he live. He is one of the dudes I took the I.D. from, but he don't be at that place 'bout once or twice. We already checked it out," Fingers said.

"We know exactly where the apartment is off MLK too," Cee Cee said.

"That nigga Tony got to go," Ant said.

As we sat there going over the pros and cons to an immediate response, Rock walked in.

"They scared as motherfuckers. Oh, they gonna come out," Rock said.

"Yo, Rock, they said they know who shot Julius. Why don't me and you go get this motherfucker? Ant, you and Kwon go after that nigga Tony. Then lets take that apartment," I said.

"Naw, yo fuck that. We don't need a crew to take the apartment. I'll do that shit on my own," Rock said.

"I'll go with you," Wembo said.

"Naw, I don't need nobody. You'll hold me up," Rock said.

We sat all night working out a plan. We even found a role for Eagle.

"They shouldn't have no property on the south side. That apartment and any other apartments on this side must go," Don Don said.

"Oh, I'm going to shut it down," Rock said.

"Cee Cee, call our cop friend for a few favors," I said.

"That nigga Magnus might not come up for a while, but I'm gonna break that nigga to his knees," Don Don said.

The next morning, I went to see my uncle in D.C.'s Lorton Correctional Institution. When I walked in the visiting hall there were about forty men being visited. I saw a few people I knew from around the way.

When my uncle approached, he already had tears in his eyes. He was shaking, blowing his nose with one hand and holding a cane with the other.

"Damn boy," he said breathing very hard.

"It's all right unc," I said.

"No, shit not all right. Shit not all right. Them motherfuckers shot my son," he said hitting his cane on the floor tile.

"We got this unc. We gonna take care of it," I said.

"No. I need you to find out what kind of cars they drive, where they live at, who they family. I want all of them motherfuckers," he said.

"Don't worry about it."

"Want to be like me?" he said. "Look at me, I can barely move. They want me to die up in here. You don't want to be like me. All I need you to do is get that info. I got some boys coming in from out of town."

It all fell on deaf ears. We had a plan all worked out. And at this point, we didn't want anybody from the outside to mess it up.

"We got it all worked out," I said.

"Listen, you don't wanna be here. Look around. Here is no more. They shipping us up out of here, and the word is, outside wardens don't like niggas from D.C."

"I'm numb. That's all I could tell you. I'm numb to this shit. I'll get you some info, but I can't promise you nothin' else. But I tell you this," I said, looking right into his watery eyes. "We gonna get them motherfuckers."

"I want them dead nephew," he said.

We decided to lay low for three days as Julius still clung to life. While my cell phone took calls from my mother, we made sure our plans were market tight. We went over it piece by piece.

Wembo, Cee Cee, Eagle and I were going after Raftin. He was their hit man and the one who shot Julius and Larry. Rock and Fingers was going in the apartment. Ant and Kwon was going to take Tony. We all sat in the apartment the day before we were to make our move. Rock and Fingers were the only two that weren't there.

"Man, where is the Mayor at?" I asked.

"He may have heard about Julius," Cee Cee said.

Knocking on the door and coming in on high intensity, Rock said, "Look at the news. Look at the news. I fucked up their whole spot!"

"What you talkin' about?" I asked.

"I went up in there and I fucked up the spot. They won't be comin' back to the Southeast."

"I haven't seen that nigga Mag, but I'm laid uptown until I see 'em. I'm not runnin' up in no joint right now," Don Don said.

"They sleepin' on us. Fuck 'em niggas," Rock said.

"Rock, you movin' too fast," Don Don said.

"Hey, where Fingers at?" Cee Cee asked.

"That nigga got the shakes," Rock said.

"We goin' to see if we could get this nigga," Ant said, as him and Kwon got up.

"Let's meet at Hagerstown Commons after everything is done," Rock said.

We laid low until about four in the morning, and the news did report that an apartment in Southeast was raided. They found one dead and the place turned over.

Eagle was dressed as a D.C. police officer and had a vehicle with sirens. I had on a navy pea coat, black Nike boots, black jeans, black skull cap and two white tees. One of them was brand new and the other was covered with Ronald's blood.

It worked out perfect because the D.C. Police Department, in an effort to make the department more efficient, had transferred most of the Black police officers uptown and most of the white cops to the Southside, so Eagle worked out perfectly.

We sat outside Raftin's house and waited. Eagle and Cee Cee played cops while Wembo and I laid out back, but Eagle laid a block away as Cee Cee did walking rounds. Wembo and I took turns using the Bushnell binoculars. At about nine in the morning Wembo said he saw him in the back bathroom window.

"Pittsburgh, make your move," I said.

Just as I expected, as soon as Eagle knocked on the door, moments later Raftin came running out the back door. As soon as he jumped over the fence, Wembo and I were waiting for him.

"You need a ride?" I asked, as Wembo grabbed him. We put him in the car. Wembo duct taped him and we rode. We met Cee Cee and Eagle at the warehouse.

"We got this bitch nigga," I said, to Ant via the two-way.

"I be wit you in a minute. Out," Ant said.

When we got to the warehouse I told them to sit him down, take the tape off and strap him to the chair. As soon as they did that, he said, "I didn't have nothin' to do with it."

"With what?" I asked.

"Man, I didn't have nothing to do with it, man," he said.

"L, don't talk to that motherfucker. Kill his ass," Cee Cee said.

"Naw, I'm a cut his motherfuckin' ear off first. You know who you shot, huh? Do you? Huh?"

"Kill his ass," Cee Cee said.

"Where Magnus at?" I asked

"I don't know," he said.

"Eagle give me my fuckin' knife," I said. I walked right over to him and asked again.

"I don't know," he said. I grabbed his head and cut his fuckin' ear off. He screamed in agony, "New York, New York. Please, I didn't have nothing to do with it. I... please..."

"Fuck you," Cee Cee said.

Pow, pow, pow, pow, pow it sounded, as she laid five bullets in his chest.

Wembo changed and stuffed him in a bag and we rode. We went back to the street where Magnus apartment was located, looking for more drama, and to drop Raftin in the middle of the street, and drop him we did.

We dropped our gloves and other evidence, and then got on the highway straight toward Hagerstown.

"That's what that nigga get. I did that for JP and Ronald and I'll do it again," Cee Cee said.

"Ok, strong woman," Wembo said.

As we were riding, the police chief came on the news and said, "We're going to get those thugs and put them away for the rest of their lives. It makes no kind of sense for these kinds of people to be on the street. They are no good thugs."

It was like Miles Davis' Concerto De Arenjues playing as, my mood went from glad and then to sad. It was at that time I understood war and what Julius was talking about when he would say, "Think about your next battle and keep in mind winning the war is the goal." The radio had the police chief and councilmen talking about the violence. They also talked about the 'Hope 6' program, which was the engine behind tearing down project communities. "No good thugs, no good thugs. That's all," the chief said.

I didn't like to see blood spilled, but war is war and the result of battle is the lost of blood. It would have been ok if we signed up with the million dollar boys club. The thought, fight for them while they send their children to college. What the civil workers didn't understand was that some of us were born soldiers, born that way. We didn't start it. We didn't go in someone else's hood and try to take it. They killed my friend and shot my cousin. Malcolm X once said, "...It doesn't mean that I advocate violence, but at the same time I am not against violence. I don't even call it violence when it's self-defense, I call it intelligence."

By what measurements do they judge us? I wondered have they considered the deaths of Dr. King and Malcolm X closely, as they relate to the people who were left behind.

By now, we would be celebrating our freedom and our ancestors. Vowing to never forget that our forefathers were treated like human dogs and vowing to fight to the death if another man tried to rape our mothers, take our tongues and make us dumb. We would have been to Congress, the White House and the United Nations concerning our history. And the record would be for the whole world to see that Africa's American population realized that a tree has roots. There would have been a book of roots and understandings, second only to the Holy Bible in homes of African-Americans.

If only they weren't killed, we would have realized by now we come from a people who respected history and taught it to their children. They respected their grandmother's mother and they could recite generations of kin. We would have realized that we were feeding ourselves and maintaining ourselves before our cousins came from Europe.

By what measurements do they judge us? 'Defend the poor and the fatherless: do justice to the afflicted and needy.'

I read that Jesus said, "Judge not according to the appearance, but judge righteous judgments." Righteous judgments are based of fairness and understanding.

When I went to Lorton to see my uncle, I saw men in there that was hit with the one-strike rule.

Some of them were serving twenty to life because they were trying to take care of their families. One guy in there was serving ten years because he was trying to make some money for college. How is it that people who rape and hurt children get a better deal?

"Yeah?" I said, answering my phone.

"When you comin' over here?" Kim said.

"I can't make it. Somethin' came up. I be back in a few weeks," I said.

"Damn, Larnell. I told you I needed to talk with you when you got back in town," she said.

"I know, I know. Shit heavy right now."

"I'm pregnant."

"You pregnant? You said you didn't mess with dude. So how the fuck is you pregnant?"

"I don't want to hear that shit, Larnell. You know I don't fuck with nobody else."

"You not saying it's mine."

"You know what? Fuck you. You didn't wear a rubber every time. I don't need you, Larnell," Kim said as she hung the phone up.

Come on now, I thought, *Kim had plenty of male friends. But she wants to say I got her pregnant.*

Shortly after I talked with her, Ant called. "Where you at? Where you at?" he screamed. "If that nigga Rock by you, kill his ass now."

"Yo," I said, and before I could get another word out Ant interrupted.

"I got this nigga Tony squeakin'. Where you at? Don't meet that nigga Rock. He behind all this shit. All this time he got us thinkin' it was Larry, but Rock got all this shit set up."

"What the fuck you talkin' 'bout?"

I asked him to put Tony on the phone, but I couldn't understand him. He sounded like his whole face had been rearranged. Ant got back on the phone and said, "That nigga Rock. Remember, he told Steve to make the bet. All this shit started from the bet. They set it up from the bet. Him and Magnus set it all up. Listen, remember the news said they couldn't identify the body in Mag's apartment? It was Steve. They fuckin' killed Steve. It wasn't one of Mag's dudes they killed. They killed Steve. He wasn't missing."

"I don't want to hear this shit right now, got damn it!"

"He said Rock did it because Julius was trying to leave the block for the business and the studio. When I see him, I'm puttin' 'em in his head. I'm tellin' you."

"Fuck. Got damn it! Ok,ok. What you gonna do with that nigga Tony?"

"I'm 'bout to lay this motherfucker down and if I see Rock, he goin' with him," Ant said.

"It's too hot right now. Let shit cool off. I got somethin' for Rock ass. Wanna play fifty, do he? Just watch yourself and act like you don't know nothin'. I'll call him and tell him something came up. You and Kwon handle business. I'm goin' up in the mountains for a few weeks."

So, that's why Rock didn't want me to go up in the apartment with him. He had it all worked out. All this time,

I thought he was the one with good persistence. But all time, he had bad intentions, mad at Julius for trying to get to the right of the streets. That's why Julius didn't say anything about him when we were in Atlanta, but he did say he trusted Larry.

As we drove up in the mountains with its surrounding peace, I thought, it was a peace that would only last for a short time. Peace from the screaming sirens. Peace from gunfire and death every few days. Peace from the politicking civil servants. Peace from backstabbers and a world moved by ignorance. Yet, I knew I was born a soldier, and that I would return to my hood to live, love and protect 'by any means necessary.'

As Julius would say, "We got to get to the right of the streets." And once you get there, don't let your worth become your occupation. Don't let you possessions become your obsession. And don't let money become your God. Currency is for security and trading. Know that 'Ye are Gods' so said the Lord. So, conduct yourself as such. As Bob Marley and the Wailers would say, "Get up, Stand up," and always remember to "Walk like a Champion, talk like a Champion."